YOU DON'

Massimiliano Canzanella

Cover: *After dinner* by Tonia Erbino, 2017 (oil on canvas 100x70 cm)

"Somos nuestra memoria, somos ese quimérico museo de formas inconstantes, ese montón de espejos rotos."

Jorge Luis Borges

"The birds sang, the proles sang, the Party did not sing."

George Orwell

Translated from the Neapolitan by

Veronica Wilson and Massimiliano Canzanella

I

It was clear to see.

The lady filled four glasses with the red. Then she lifted one of them and took a sip from it. She bent down to take a better look at herself in the dressing-table mirror. It seemed as if she was using a finger to wipe off her wine moustache. She plugged in the stereo, switched on the radio and tuned in the first station with a decent sound quality.

She was all ears, for a song she'd never heard before. You could tell she didn't know it; she didn't know the lyrics, she'd had no time to learn them by heart.

She helped herself to another drop from a different glass. Despite the tune not being over, by now she'd already moved on to the next one. It was one she knew inside out, even though she much preferred the words, as the music couldn't keep up with her high spirits.

She turned up the volume and her tipsy voice too, oblivious to being off-key. While prancing around the room, she took a gulp from each of the four glasses, leaving lipstick marks on the rims like relics of her mouth.

She gradually became more distinct than the singer on the radio, whose timbre, in the absence of an aerial, had grown unnaturally raspy.

The doorbell rang and the singing stopped.

She glanced at the clock but couldn't tell the time. She darted into the kitchen and perused the shelves.

The visitors fidgeted a little bit longer with the chime and, before she could shut the fridge with her right buttock, they were already banging on the reinforced door, making a resonating rattle.

After ruffling the tablecloth to one side, she pulled the corkscrew out of the cutlery drawer and proceeded to unsheathe it and push it into position. She ran to the bedroom, where a sea breeze was blowing before the windows of the first-floor apartment, and she laid the cold bottle on the nightstand.

She slowly made her way to the sunless hall. Then, before dislodging the chain latch, she resumed her bubbly singalong. The tune and lyrics had won her over, as if the raucous-voiced radio had meant to keep it going so she would feel protected, safely enveloped in a familiar theme.

It was a completely different story now. She was no longer crying out to anyone who might be walking past her palazzo. Her performance standard, in fact, had improved surprisingly by sticking to the tempo and attuning to the melody. She was paying her respects to the pace of the music that bore the words, the words she loved beyond sanity, the words that could dissipate every single drop of her blood and overwhelm her.

In stepped three men, who removed their grey trench coats and chucked their unfolded and soaked brollies on the floor. They took her to the bedroom and sat her down close, then they took turns to kiss her, never crowding her. One man would tug at her chin until her face made way for the next one. And all the while she granted them permission. She let them peck her wine-reddened cheeks.

She was allowing herself to be inundated with pinching kisses from one and then another man, like the page of a music sheet being flicked back and forth ad infinitum.

The three men started to undress, but they did not remove everything. Signora Consiglia suddenly found herself completely naked. It was obvious, how the lady made her living.

II

D ue to her old age and general frailty, if she'd found out she would have never been able to live with it.

She'd been confined to a wheelchair that morning, at such an early hour, with her daughters still asleep, when her femur decided to call it a day.

It cracked up, it broke in two like a time-worn cotton reel. With the embroidered towel still clenched in her spasming hand, Giuseppina fell off the bidet and banged her head against the chilling floor tiles. She received a bump on her forehead, but meanwhile something else had become much more apparent: the elderly mother was destined to rot on that trundling catafalque, waiting for the Almighty to come and haul her ass out of it.

Surgery was out of the question due to her sickly heart.

The anaesthetic-induced sleep might have resulted in an untimely end at the hands of the doctors. She had to muster her strength. It didn't matter whether she was going to have to hang on for a year or two, or even ten or twenty. Giuseppina couldn't move from that second-hand chair that floundered around on all fours – four squirming and squalling wheels rusted to the core. She wasn't allowed to move until "Lord Alright Jack!" would come and manhandle her, for only he had such imponderable strength.

The truth was out of bounds to Giuseppina Lopez, for she would certainly have died as a direct result of it, with her lifeless body possibly leading to the death of her three grief-stricken daughters, who took care of their mother day and night without any notion of respite.

They would prepare many a flavoursome meal to sugar-coat their mother's palate, constantly soured by the shed-load of pills she had to take every hour. Every single morning they would toilet, bathe and dress their mother, with the dirty clothes heading straight into the washing machine, and then out on the internal balcony of the close where they were hung to dry. All in the presence of their neighbours, who watched their every move while revering their exemplary conduct, one that God should have rewarded with the longest possible life.

The wrung-out laundry was hoisted onto the washing lines by means of wooden pegs, the "real thing" when it comes to getting the hanging job done. The plasticky ones they sell nowadays come with floppy springs that invariably come loose. And if you were to try and fix them ... nah, it wouldn't be worth the bother! You'd only be wasting your time, really.

The way her daughters saw it, if their mum had been kept in the dark, it would hardly have been their fault. On the eve of their family ordeal – a mess greater than the three sisters' worst nightmares combined – Giuseppina received a visit from a niece who had the uttermost devotion to her old aunt, and whom she resolutely intended to protect from any further suffering. Lina, short for Pasqualina, didn't want her to experience any worse hell-like torment than her ailing health. Therefore she came up with a story, a tiny little fib that, in her mind, would have been completely safe. In actual fact, that same white lie would have contributed to relieving her auntie's malaise.

After entering the dining room, Lina found herself with a letter planted in her hands – bad news that the elderly lady's daughters read while their lashing tears deluged their aprons. Her cousins had hoped she might have come up with a smart plan. Or, at least, smarter than their not entirely constructive alternative –peeing their pants.

Their little brother, their mother Giuseppina's only male son, had fallen – killed in combat by a grenade that had detonated right next to him. The letter detailed how the soldier had died instantly,

... painlessly, and without feeling a thing.

"Aunt, something's happened. He's fine, mind! He's in hospital; they took him to the military clinic but they should send him home within the week, alright?"

Without even hearing her son's name, Giuseppina immediately understood: her niece was alluding to her son Luigi – the baby who'd come along when she was already a lady of a certain age. When, since her daughters had not married, and given that no one in the house was in need of any nanas or grannies, she made a vow to the Holy Virgin Mary, who had to let her be a mother again.

The thing was, she said: "I still feel it in me. I can make it." And so it happened that, around her fiftieth birthday, she bore Luigi who caused his mum plenty of sleepless nights.

As a matter of fact, that baby was brought about by a vow. And now, with her boy lying in a hospital bed, Giuseppina looked at once into a new one: a brand-new vow she would make to the Virgin Mary there and then. To the *Madonna*.

Was she going to be any good, though? After all, she had lost her only child, by coldheartedly having him crucified right before her eyes, and without deigning to intervene. Could Giuseppina truly believe in her, in the face of such a daunting premise? Was she to have full faith in a woman who hadn't taken a single step to save her dying baby son? If she had refused to help her own child, how was she ever going to move her fat butt now? The lazy cow! Forget it.

The Holy Virgin. That stupid good-for-nothing. She was deemed a worthless woman, deserving only a spit in the face. Giuseppina hawked and spat at her, though her gob remained well off-target.

Lina tried to reassure her, for truly there was no need to be worrying. The military clinic where Luigi had been admitted was as comfortable as a five-star hotel.

The niece dried the slobber off her auntie's fuming countenance, while the old woman carried on muttering the foulest epithets and cursed "that big whore!" for not stepping in to deflect the grenade.

She vehemently requested the little portrait nailed to the wall behind the rosewood headboard. Yet, when she held the Virgin Mary in her hands and looked the childless mother closely in the eyes, the old woman desisted, bringing the swearing to a chilling halt. But she demanded, without making any crap excuses, that she watch over her son's steps on the path to recovery.

She also expected the Madonna to keep vigil at night, meaning every night until his release from hospital.

The Holy Virgin had to have mercy on Giuseppina. She just had to! The lady in the light blue mantle had shed the grace of a son on her. And now, by the same token, it was her duty to keep an eye on the boy wounded by the shrapnel that she, and nobody but her, had failed to intercept.

In the end, she didn't want to spit at her, not in her face nor anywhere else, considering the lady was still weeping. It was two thousand years since she had cried over her son's passing, and yet the Holy Virgin's grief appeared as the crudeness of a recent loss.

Truth be told, before that morning Giuseppina had never paid much attention to the little portrait, and never once had those soundless tears caught her eye.

The elderly mother kissed the frame intensely and then clasped it to her chest, as they wept and felt close all at once, dead close to another. As if the mother of Jesus, the Holy Virgin Mary, were a younger sister whom Giuseppina could have never left alone or hurt in any way.

Because the woman – poor Christ! – had actually lost her son.

Inconceivable, right?

Well, thankfully, her boy was still very much alive.

Fine. It was true! He was in hospital with a few minor injuries. Still, all Giuseppina had to do to see him again, as promised in the latest bulletin provided by her niece, was hang on a couple of weeks. After which time, Luigi would reappear at her side, possibly with a bunch of flowers and a get-well card for her beautiful *mama*.

No problem, a couple of weeks. She could set her heart on it.

*

Lina's stories had almost completely calmed her nerves, so much so that at lunch she cleared her plate.

The second she dozed off, however, slumped in the atrocious constraint of her wheelchair, Giuseppina was roused by an absolute racket that, from the adjacent dining room, stormed inside her room. Mirrors, or perhaps windowpanes, being smashed to pieces; maniacal shrieks, and the kind of berserk fits you would only witness in a lunatic asylum. She thought she could discern the groaning of flagellants raging against themselves, as well as the echo of the most strident wailing she had ever heard.

Giuseppina didn't get it. What was that moaning about now? What were her daughters beating themselves up for, if Luigi was really due to be released from hospital within a few days? To clear up any aggravating doubts, she begged her devoted niece Lina, who had simply popped round for a placid sit-down with her best auntie and wise buddy, to urgently summon those three idiots that were her cousins, since their well pissed-off mum needed to have a serious word with them.

On seeing them enter her room, Giuseppina barely recognised what appeared to be the remnants of her daughters. A triptych of Lazarus, with the youngest one presenting her cheeks and temples covered in crimson scratches, while her older sister's eyeballs were jutting out of their orbits, and the eldest's knees were steeped in blood, with her legs caught in a Charleston-induced hysteria.

Instead of holding only one sibling mainly responsible, at that point Giuseppina blamed the entire incident on the lot of them. On all three, who had overreacted equally about their little brother being in hospital for no good reason. And she swore that, if it weren't for that "Mean Heavenly Father" who had forsaken her in that bloody trap of a chair, "by Jesus Almighty-Fuck-Him", besides the cuts and bruises they had already caused to themselves, she would have finished them off with a proper battering.

It was a matter of days.

"What the heck is wrong with you?"

If she, Luigi's mother, had been able to control her agitation, then who could have possibly given them the right? Who on earth had given, to those three hideous spinsters, the right to make such a scene?

"Who do you actually think you are?"

As if her failure in wreaking havoc meant that she wasn't suffering a great deal for that poor son of hers.

"It's not like he's by himself. Are you having a laugh?"

Had they already forgotten, or were they perhaps completely in the dark? Unaware of how the Virgin Mary would be staying by her son's bedside.

The two mothers, as it had previously emerged during one of Giuseppina's mystical reveries, had come to an amiable agreement. The lady in the light blue mantle from the little portrait above the headboard would be taking responsibility for the night shifts. And during her stint she wouldn't even dare take her eyes off her son.

It was an awkward conundrum. Even if Luigi's sisters had claimed their family right to look after their little brother, they wouldn't have been allowed anywhere near the ward anyway. Regardless. Three middle-aged women in a hospital for male patients only? Not a chance. Whereas the Holy Virgin would have easily been allowed to stay. To stay through the night, in the same room where men might have been getting a quick wash – naked as jaybirds – before getting dried and dressed in their pyjamas again. Where aching soldiers might have been whining quietly to avoid making a ludicrous spectacle of themselves.

She who had been watching and crying over her dead son for over two thousand years, the lady in the blue mantle, could well stay. For sure.

*

The next morning, Giuseppina awoke around six. Despite not having slept a wink, save a couple of relatively tranquil hours, jammed between a watch and a sentry duty, she felt as if she'd laid dormant for years. And, though completely dazed, she had a few whims in urgent need of attention. Firstly, from Emilia, who had brought her a sturdier pillow, along with a cup of full-bodied espresso coffee, she demanded to know whether Luigi had returned. And if he hasn't "I want to know why!" she burst out in a huff.

Giuseppina carefully marked every word that came out of her daughter's mouth. There were six more days to wait, which for someone like her, who had never been the patient kind, were going to be no easy ride. She had to learn a little self-restraint, and quickly too. She could have let herself be transfixed by the spike-shaped arms of the gold-lacquer clock that rested under the glass dome, where it kept count of every moment with the help of Roman numerals.

In other words, the poor-quality favour from when she'd got married.

A largely oxidised pendulum, with four metal spheres at its extremity, provided the clock's mechanism with the necessary thrust to keep going, so that the time that had to pass could effectively continue. Exactly what Giuseppina had to find now, a way to pass the time, so that days and nights would move along. That week or two, or was it three now?

13

She couldn't tell. She couldn't remember for the life of her. Although what occurred to her next were the exact words spoken with a forked tongue by her affectionate niece.

"Sweetheart, I don't get this. Will you tell me what's going on?" asked Giuseppina, two days after Lina had informed her discombobulated auntie of her son's "predicament".

The misunderstanding was ultimately attributed to the elderly woman's poor hearing. Lina had already explained it to her. How Luigi had to undergo therapy which woud take up to a month. Likewise, she reminded her of how military hospitals tend to prolong the stay of their patients well beyond their real needs, so they can milk a few extra bucks for their budgets.

It was a matter of thirty days or so, that was all.

*

At nine in the morning on the third day, Giuseppina's eldest daughter, Vicenza, The Immaculate One, as sardonically nicknamed by her mum, the one compelled to tidy up even though there was nothing to clear away, and who was also to blame – as determined by her angry sisters – for the loss of a photo album crammed with snapshots of their dad, which the obsessive freak was highly suspected to have dumped in the bin, for she could not tolerate it in a place other than its ordained location, entered the bedroom with a wet cloth, two old sheets from an old newspaper, and a plastic bottle of white spirit.

Giuseppina pleaded for the clock's dome to be left as it was, with the fingermarks smeared all over it. She knew very well how terrible her eldest could be, with cleanliness and order being two categorical imperatives. So, the elderly mother reiterated her appeal three more times. Hoping that her spartan daughter would let the glass be until Luigi's return home. After all, it was a matter of thirty days. Then, on the boy's return, she could have scrubbed it and polished it inside and out any way she liked.

"Goodness' sake, ma!" Vicenza exclaimed in utter disgust, as the mere sight of the glass dome covered in greasy sweat made her skin crawl. Besides, how did her mum know for sure that Luigi would be coming back in exactly one month's time?

As her daughter tore the plastic cap of the glass dome open, Giuseppina was once again reminded of how health beaureaucrats operated in those days, greasing the hospital beds' wheels in any way they could and, in the process, turning – just like that – a month's stay into two, and then three.

And that's if everything went to the doctors' plan.

"By the time they've done every possible test..." sighed The Immaculate One, as the exposed clock made itself heard through its baritone tick-tock. A soporific din that caused instantaneous drowsiness.

Once she'd finished drying it with an entire page from an old broadsheet, Vicenza gingerly craned the beautifully scented dome back into position, like the newly fitted see-through drawbridge of an impregnable moated castle.

The dome smelled of white spirit, just like the hospital room Giuseppina remembered from when she had her varicose veins removed. Surely, her son's room would have smelt just the same. No doubt. Military nurses, she had heard, are very well known for their uncompromising approach toward hygiene. Some say that unless their wards are spick and span, there is no way they will put their dusters and mops down.

Sixty days or so.

She had to hang on another couple of months, maybe three at the most, before she could see her baby son again, who would have found himself sleeping in a hospital bed for the very first time. On the day she gave birth to him, in fact, Giuseppina refused to stay the night. She signed a voluntary discharge form where, in case of future complications, she relinquished her right to take any future legal action against the hospital board. She took off with her newborn baby lapped in a mixed-wool shawl, like a pup she had chosen from the cages of an animal shelter.

"He's going to stay in that bleeding hospital for about three months ... alright then, that means he'll be able to give me the occasional call, right? Come on ... It's not like he's paralysed ... He's only waiting on the consultants to run a few routine tests ... X-rays, blood samples, blood pressure ... The usual checks that need to be done before a patient can be sent home again..."

The three daughters listened, captivated by their elderly mum's expostulations.

She was spot-on.

A telephone call, free of charge too, was an entitlement reserved to all soldiers injured on the front line, for a call home is a symbolic token of the unwavering gratitude and courtesy owed to all men willing to make the ultimate sacrifice for their country. Moreover, if you happened to be in the most desolate or remote of all places, the soldiers who were not on their feet were given plenty of opportunities to write home. With their letters bearing an air-mail sticker on the top-right-hand corner.

Every morning, there is a plane whose route is centred on the delivery of all letters written by soldiers wounded in battle. Words of nostalgia and undiminished love ultimately slipped right into the laps of their anxious mothers at home. Alongside the petrified hands of fathers, wives and children, who look up to the sky in the hope it might bring plenty of fresh news.

"Hold on, a little bit longer!" whisper the exasperated folks who hang about the windowpanes all day.

But now, you'll never guess what happened next.

It was one-thirty in the afternoon, and the three sisters were busy setting the table for lunch.

Giuseppina was intent on peering into the chink of clear sky above the rooftops across the street, a mere stone's throw from her bedroom. She was trying to catch a glimpse of the plane laden with thousands of fluttering letters written by homesick young men like her son, when out of the blue came a telephone call from Luigi. It didn't last long. What was it, a minute? Half, perhaps? Whatever. How was the elderly woman supposed to know anyway?

As they lowered the phone into her gnarled hands, she clearly heard the voice of someone calling out "Ma!" And that was more than enough for Giuseppina's cry to finally burst the banks of her forbearance. She wept and wept until her tears were dammed yet again by the arrival of a pill and a glass of tap water.

Not once had she ever managed to swallow that frigging blue pellet in a downer. It invariably got stuck somewhere in her throat. A separate amount of water, this time aimed at relieving the ghastly drought of her entire mouth, was soon handed over to her by her second daughter Patrizia, who wiped the bottom of the glass with an ironed dish towel, mindfully lifted from a stack inside the linen cupboard, where the perfectly aligned rows of clean laundry were regimented by The Immaculate One in the most draconian fashion.

Soon Patrizia led her mum to the room next door, where her lunch would be served. She only arrested the chair when she was satisfied with the angle, the trajectory that would secure her mum's safe re-entry to the homely atmosphere of the round dinner table. Next, she put the brakes on the front wheels and laid a red and white squared cotton napkin on her lap, while a piping hot plate switched off its thrusters and touched down on the wine-stained tablecloth.

All five women were sat around the table. Lina did not want to touch a thing. In the most dexterous of apologies, she complained of how the poorly digested steak from the previous night had caused her some horrendous bloatedness and heartburn.

Her aunt Giuseppina wasn't feeling that hungry either. She was still thinking about how she hadn't had a real chance to fully enjoy her son's call. She didn't have a clue what had happened there. Plus, now she was worried Luigi might not call ever again. She'd been soft enough to give in to her tears, and in future her conscientious boy might have simply thought of protecting his silly mum from the risky palpitations. He was aware of his mum's heart condition, and therefore conscious of its inability to deal with any twists and turns.

19

"Meat for dinner is too heavy on the stomach," Giuseppina reminded her indisposed niece, who ever since that day refused point blank to play the part, to pretend that she was Luigi; to act as though she were the son who was getting in touch with his distressed mother.

"Never again … Forget it!" admonished Lina as she made her way back from the upstairs neighbour, who had put her phone line, along with her whole apartment, at the bereft women's disposal.

"I would appreciate if you would not involve me in any repeats of this tragicomedy – what an absolute misery!" She made herself even clearer, while avoiding raising the tone of her voice too much, given that regret about the stupid farce was already splattered all over the three sisters' mortified faces.

With or without a handkerchief pressed against her mouth, anyone would have been able to tell the bloody difference. And it was only because of her rampant sobbing that the elderly mother had not found out the whole truth.

"Do you think she's an idiot?" scolded Lina under her breath, for the three sisters' idea of a "surprise call home" from their dead brother had been completely fucked-up from the very beginning.

III

Despite being one of those splendid mid-September days, not much could be seen because of the sheets hung out to dry from the upstairs neighbour's balcony, which intermittently concealed her lascivious figure in sync with the gusts of torrid wind.

Signora Consiglia sat in the kitchen, her legs resting on a chair rocked in the direction of the small window, while her nail-polished feet lolled serenely. She had some cheek, to be living the life of the working girl with her teenage daughter's bedroom being right opposite to hers.

She had separated from her husband, or so they were told – the select few who'd heard the story from her lips. Her alibi, however, was disproved every time by the verdict of her hawk-eyed neighbours, who knew perfectly well how her husband had chucked her. He had dumped her straight off and left her in dire straits, without even cash to get the shopping.

The lone mother did her best to man up as if nothing major had happened. And a few hours after her husband had left the house, along with a suitcase packed with his most beloved clothes and toiletries, she got dressed and walked to her daughter's school to attend a crucial parents' evening, during which she would have been kept up to speed about the girl's most pressing needs for improvement.

Signora Consiglia was clearly strong-willed enough to be the breadwinner, the undaunted captain who would have kept the house afloat through a perfect storm such as the one unleashed by the drastic change in her family circumstances.

When dealing with uncharted parental problems such as her daughter's period, she also had to learn how to split her persona into innumerable parts, all adhering to her new comprehensive role of chief-in- command of the household. She had to start acting not only as a mother but also as a friend and confidant, a buddy with whom her daughter would have shared everything, including the most intimate aspects of her sprouting puberty. Occasionally she was both man and woman, as well as mother, father and friend. Like a ubiquitous deity capable of seeing, hearing and divining all cognisable things. Anything at all.

"Why did she decide to be a working girl, though?" delved Giuseppina from her observation point across the street. What was the real problem behind such an extreme choice? Did she perhaps want to seize the day and have a little fun, an attempt to follow in her husband's debauched footsteps?

Her husband, an emeritus prick who had nonchalantly resigned from all his duties and chores, including his basic and most natural parental obligation as father.

What a piece of shit... A sleazy bastard who would not contribute to the household expenses with a penny, and who spent most nights chasing girls who looked as young as his daughter.

By living the life of the working girl, perhaps the lady across the street was trying to grab life with all the perks of the senses – all the *being* she had missed out on thus far.

Whatever and whoever that *being* might *be*.

She couldn't have cared less about who they really were, those men. Those men that were never the same. Those men who were always *other ones*. Those who punctually turned up in threes and that, once in the hall, took off their trench coats and nestled around her with their pants on, for each one was too embarrassed to appear naked in the presence of the other two.

Whether it was through one of the windows or by keeping a steady eye on the bedroom balcony, you could easily tell. How the lady enjoyed watching the men arrive outside her palazzo before they made their way past the portal door.

They came in, never to cross that very same threshold again. Inducing some to believe – those who were unaware of the backstreet alley – that she regurgitated her visitors once she'd had her fair share of fun with them. Or even, according to a less forgiving myth, that she kept those bodies for good, after she had wolfed them in one ravenous go.

IV

She was still trying to figure out a way to pass those few days that separated her from her son. A counter-attack measure to retaliate the nasty blows inflicted by time.

"Bloody bossy boots!"

From under the glass dome, the gold-lacquer clock kept bullying her. It nudged and nipped at Giuseppina, making her stagger and fall in a chasm under the weight of her ebbing physical vigour.

Her daughters kept telling her, she couldn't be thinking about her boy every minute of the day. Luigi's health had to get a little bit better still. Then, once all the tests from this world had certified his full recovery, the army would send him back home for good on account of his previous wound in action.

Her poor son's tribulations would soon be over.

But then again, how could she be so sure? Whether they took the boy's harrowing medical record into consideration or not, who could tell her with absolute certainty that the army would have not snatched him away from her for a second time?

To dispel such a daunting scenario, the smart old woman swiftly came up with a back-up plan.

On the fourth day since the onset of her son's "discomfort", in the early hours of a sweltering afternoon, the priest bustled inside her bedchamber and provided Giuseppina with all sorts of reassurances. Yes, okay, alright! He would agree to have Luigi hidden in the crypt.

Now, it might well be that she'd failed in averting the grenade that tossed her son into the air like a ball of hay; nevertheless Giuseppina, after much consideration, resolved to focus on one more positive and unquestionable fact: Luigi's life had been saved by the same semi-negligent hand of the Madonna, who had diverted the boy's fall towards an area where the fluffy grass guaranteed a substantially harmless landing. And on the basis of this direct intervention by the Holy Virgin, nobody, Ministry of Camorra included, no one could dream of arrogating the right to redeploy her son anywhere near the combat zone, even though her son had joined the army as a volunteer.

Moreover, any refusal to comply with this view would represent an open violation of the scheme laid down by the Madonna to best protect her son; a blasphemous affront, given that the Ministry had no right to obstruct the Lady's will in any way.

Ergo, Father Guglielmo had to hide him away in the crypt. Or else he too would have been contravening the Virgin's commands, which would have been an even greater paradox.

The thing was, as the grinning priest began to elucidate, for the benefit of the elderly lady whose naivety had struck his most pitiful chords, there was no real need to worry.

"Signora Lopez, first and foremost you ought to think about your own wellbeing!"

Apparently, there wasn't going to be any way to hide anyone, let alone her virtually veteran son.

"By the time Luigi gets back, within a few months or so, war will be a distant memory!" said the clergyman.

In his opinion, the war had dragged on for too long, and the end of it all was nigh beyond question; the time when men would be made to look at themselves right in the eyes, and judge the true extent of their worth. All those contemptible men who had lost every sense of dignity were soon going to be reacquainted with their beleaguered conscience.

Day in, day out, you would read a new story in the paper about a church or a tabernacle where an effigy of *The Mother of All Mothers* had been caught in the act of shedding an unspecified number of tears. How much longer did she have to weep? How many more tears had to gush out of her torn soul, before they understood, before those worthless men could see their nothingness and end this ungodly carnage.

Once she had mentally prepared herself for the confession of her sins, Giuseppina earnestly drew the priest's attention to the little portrait above the headboard, as she took care to point out how that Virgin Mary in a light blue mantle was crying her heart out too.

"I swear I'd never realised!" said Giuseppina candidly.

She was the first to admit it, possibly due to the simple fact of not paying the necessary attention.

"Neither had I!" interjected Father Guglielmo.

Despite having sat in that same bedroom hundreds of times, not once had he ever noticed. How that holy creature, who in this cheap transfiguration looked very much like a hot chick from the countryside, had two teeny tears stamped on her rather bony cheeks. Impossible to appreciate with the naked eye because, except for a practically imperceptible glint, the remaining part of the watery surface had been painted with the exact same colour as the rest of her pinkish skin.

*

Giuseppina wanted to be reconciled with her inner peace. But in order to properly join in the spirit – the friendly ghost of the Eucharist that currently dwelled inside the priest's briefcase – first she had to confess all her sins. Her sins... But what sort of malefaction could an elderly woman in an aggrieved condition such as hers ever commit? An irresistibly sweet old lady; a cloistered nun; a recluse who spent her days on a clanking chair, willy nilly. Which inequity could she have possibly perpetrated, since her whole existence had been put on hold by her son's injury? None, really. Except that the elderly woman's fervent brain had muddled the sacred with the profane, to the point where one of her mental juxtapositions had forged a sinful dream of the worst kind, one in which the Holy Virgin lent her face to a *working girl.*

To make herself perfectly understood, before anything else Giuseppina had to introduce Father Guglielmo to the obscene character of signora Consiglia – the harlot from across the street. The mother of a teenage daughter who regularly rendezvoused with trios of undressed men, without any qualms or the minimum decency to draw the blinds shut before she did a striptease herself.

"Trios?" snorted the priest befuddledly.

"That's right, Father. Three at the time!" sniggered Giuseppina.

The issue did not lie as much in the woman's lustfulness as, more pressingly at this time, with her bestial face having been surrogated by the celestial expression of the Holy Virgin, the mother whose existence was determined only by the tears cried over her son's death.

Why did God have to conjure up such a bizarre dream in her feeble mind, leading Giuseppina into the temptation of committing an unwanton sin? And besides, could a sin be unwanton in the first place?

Father Guglielmo initially got rather indignant, then he did his best to suppress his growing outrage and presented the elderly woman in search of penance with his most unambiguous "No, signora Lopez. Absolutely not!".

For every single occurrence signifies a miniscule and unique part of the Lord's master plan. The Almighty certainly does not improvise, nor does He ever bungle with people's lives. And since everything happens by means of the Signore's will, the dream about the lady across the street too, the dream about signora Consiglia bearing the image of the Holy Virgin, was a specific emanation of His grander schemes. God our Lord is always in the right, and for this simple and equally magnificent reason nothing can ever be the product of chance.

"Imagine the chaos if what you are suggesting were even remotely possible!" lambasted the priest.

Having learnt the fundamental precept of the Lord being infallible, now Giuseppina felt she could confess the remainder of her sin. She spilt the beans about holding the Holy Virgin personally responsible, liable for not diverting the course of the grenade that had temporarily confined Luigi to a hospital bed. And she let the cat out of the bag about her summarily sentencing the Madonna to being cursed and spat at.

The elderly mother did not even omit the disgraceful detail of how her attempt to gob at the portrait had miserably failed, not to mention her chin being spattered with drool.

On hearing this last detail, Father Guglielmo emitted a shrill cry of elation. By the inspiration of God, he thought he'd got to the bottom of this unearthly sacrilege.

"Right, I've got it!" declared the clergyman.

Essentially, signora Lopez had dreamt of the Holy Virgin being a whore because, through her previous profanation of the little portrait above the headboard, the elderly woman had effectively soiled the Madonna's candour.

"An attempted sin is still a sin, you know?"

Giuseppina's inconsistent spit had missed the target, but the wickedness of her gesture had not gone unnoticed by the ever-present Lord.

This whole sticky situation could finally be put to rest. Father Guglielmo could easily see how it had all been possible. The holy image of the Mother of God had been covered in dirt and reduced to scum until her sacred head, in the old woman's dream, had been projected over the neck of a woman who instead was synonymous with dirt.

"Being considered *a priori* the filthiest woman of all," continued the priest, "it is not hard to understand how to you, signora Lopez, this pitiful individual that goes by the name of Consiglia has eventually come to represent the worst idea of human filth imaginable."

That was precisely what the clergyman thought had happened. Giuseppina's nasty dream meant that, even though she had not given a helping hand to deviate the grenade's course, the Holy Virgin was not a dirty woman. The Mother of God was not a slut. She was no bitch, and she did not deserve to be showered in spit like that.

"See for yourself, Father. She's just buzzed another three of them in. Did you see that?" Giuseppina asked fretfully.

The priest kept his eyes well away from the palazzo's portal. All those tales of carnal desecration had given him a tell-tale hard-on that put him in a terribly awkward position. He was currently busy with the ostensorium in one hand and the holy bread in the other, which prevented him from adjusting his trousers and thereby declotting his lubricious groin. Then he quelled the old bag's jabbering with the holy bread and set about gathering his blessed stuff.

Father Guglielmo was about to leave, and chanted his *"Arrivederci, signora Lopez!"*, when he heard a song rising from the vestibule and cross all the way to the old woman's chamber. The sweetest music, accompanied by the most melodious voice he'd ever known. Pure harmony soaked in a lily-petal scent. A distinctly pervasive fragrance, altogether identical to another one he still remembered vividly, from the day he took his parish on a coach pilgrimage to Lourdes. He felt it while bathing in the sanctuary's pool. It was a marvellous and exceptionally beautiful *profumo*. An enveloping bliss that numbed your senses until you felt languid and heavy-eyed.

"She must love it to bits," smirked Giuseppina. "Lately she's been listening to this one non-stop... always the same tune – over and over again!"

The clergyman left the apartment on the second floor while the voice of the lady from across the street inundated the ramps of stairs beneath his inebriated tread. Moments later, he clambered out of the building and landed on the sun-baked pavement, while showing the clear symptoms of delirium; the working girl from the first-floor apartment was yodelling the same Neapolitan air she seemed to adore through and through.

Father Guglielmo kept his head down. He crossed the road and stationed himself by the palazzo's buzzer. The tenants' family names were nowhere to be seen. Plus, all he knew was her first name, Consiglia.

Esposito? Borriello? Imparato? Iovine?

Who was most likely to be the big whore?

He pressed a random button. But as soon as the red light of the live video connection came on, the man of the cloth pulled himself backwards and set off in a panic. He didn't want to be in the picture, fearing the buzzer might hide the camera of another dirty film.

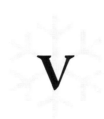

V

Nearly a month went by, before Giuseppina's *little man*, as his mummy still loved to call him, was loaded onto a plane full of youngsters who had all shared in their country's vision of the future. Luigi and another whole bunch of kids were sent back home stuffed in coffins that were barely recognisable, disguised as they were by a tricolour rag that the army had fiercely imposed on all fallen in battle.

In order to make it to their little brother's funeral, the three sisters had to take it in turns – fifteen minutes each. They used a rota system so their mum wouldn't be left on her own at any time. If she'd noticed or even sensed her daughters' absence, she might have kicked off. Giuseppina could have churned out further questions, more reasonable and plausible interrogatives about her son's "protracted absence".

The entire district had thronged to salute the soldiers returned to their block in more than one piece. At the foot of the altar of the Basilica of *Santa Maria della Sanità*, the coffins were disposed in a single row across the nave, while the tight-knit mourners rocked back and forth before an unflinching Father Guglielmo.

Some of the relatives strongly wanted a private function, though the Ministry of Camorra couldn't have been any clearer with them: the state would have footed the bill only on condition that the exact same service be provided to all families.

The diktat which prohibited the public use of 'commemoration tools' also extended to the customisation of soldiers' coffins by means of pictures or nameplates. Their faces were allegedly expendable, including the riveting eyes of the dead. The one thing of paramount importance was that the fire of war raged inside the young soldiers' hearts, and that in the process this same inferno licked up their eyes and minds. Before the mourners' knees were bent by the unbearable sight of their loss, whoever entered the church had to refer to the sergeant on duty in the vestibule, whose flipboard was then brandished to mark the path along the aisles. Once arrived at the designated pew, the warrant officer walked up to the line of coffins. Next, with his biro pen, he would indicate the exact spot – the exact dead person that the relatives' tears should be aimed at.

To make matters worse, quite often the sergeant would make a complete mess of his print-outs, resulting in the mourners looking in completely the wrong direction, and with their tears and sighs gone to waste completely.

One at a time, the three sisters walked past the holy-water font, dipping two or three of their right-hand fingertips, before they shuffled to their seats. Sitting next to them was a young man whom they did not recognise. A young chap who was evidently sobbing in the direction of their brother's remains, as broken-heartedly as only a secret sibling could have done. By the flapping of his lips, you could also surmise that he was continually mumbling Luigi's name, as if that one word were the only one left in his prayers.

He was likely to be a comrade from the same company as their brother's. Though dressed in civilian clothes, he had both the shaven head and the abysmal bags under the eyes of a recently furloughed man. The rest of his face was moist with all the tears he'd been forced to smother, for a weepy combatant would have breached the common view of a good patriot's warring mind.

It was as if the exact same introduction scene were rehearsed three consecutive times within the forty-five minutes of the funeral ceremony.

"I'm Nunzio. A friend of Luigi's. We fought together."

"I'm Emilia, his sister."

"I'm Patrizia, his sister."

"I'm Vicenza, his sister."

"Were you with him when he passed?"

"I was right next to him. To be honest, I don't know how he could possibly die without both of us sharing the same fate."

"Well, that's life, isn't it?" replied the three sisters resignedly.

To respect the agreed fifteen-minute slot, the first two sisters had to scrape themselves from the pew so that they would not be late. More importantly they had to give a chance to the third and last attendee, who was already in position outside the palazzo. From where she ran to the toilets of the sacristy, got changed into her mourning clothes and darted towards the parvis steps.

Nunzio courteously led each of the three women out into the churchyard. And it was here that Vicenza, the last appointed masquerader, invited her brother's comrade upstairs for a cup of coffee.

Later, of course.

Oh, heavens! Much later...

I mean when it was all done and dusted. When the pall-bearers had finished carrying Luigi and the rest of the fallen youths. Once they had paraded the dead along the teeming nave, and unloaded them into the boot of a twenty-five-year-old Mercedes. The spluttering alloy-wheeled station wagons were double-parked on the pavement, in the piazza where hundreds of apparently wound-up folks clapped sonorously. Like child automatons marking the dramatic finale of an epic puppet show.

The cortège? God forbid, they had been banned from time immemorial. In the view of the Ministry of Camorra, a corpse on the move may have caused an outbreak of sadness.

*

Nunzio had been invited by all three sisters, who had taken an identical decision. Well, this is how it worked, in reality: Emilia had the initial thought, which was emphatically praised by Patrizia and conclusively approved by Vicenza.

He wasn't even given a chance to get a whiff of coffee. Instead, the three bereaved women took their brother's comrade into the dining room, where they immediately began to tell him about their poor old mother.

"Of any of this, you see... of this massive misery... she doesn't have a bleeding clue. Can you believe it?"

The three sisters said it had been all because of their nosey cousin. A selfish niece who'd demanded her aunt be shielded from a lethal discovery, with the only aim of protecting herself from the devastating loss of the woman who'd been just like a mother to her.

Nunzio looked at the letter purposefully placed right in the middle of the round table, the spot commonly occupied by an empty fruit bowl which in this instance had been shifted further out, next to a hand-painted ceramic ash-tray picturing an idyllic cove from somewhere on the Amalfi coast, where the *azzurro* of a mythical sea twinkled toward the lushness of the terraced gardens of lemon trees. Notwithstanding the noticeable cracks and shards, the practical souvenir had a purely ornamental function, since the day when cigarettes too had made it onto the list of unaffordable luxuries dictated by the Citizenhip Income Board.

Without going into the cringeworthy details of the make-believe telephone call, the women explained to the young shaven-headed soldier how they had done everything they physically could to keep their mum entertained with as many tales as they could concoct.

However, too much time had passed, far too long since their mum had last heard any news of her son. Of her boy who, in her own understanding, was doing just fine in a hospital that was the bees' knees.

They didn't know where to turn any more. Their mum's inquisitiveness – "She never shut up, man!" – was honestly driving them round the bend. The relentless questioning was Chinese torture: *"Why won't his superiors let him send a single letter home? And why won't he give his mum a quick ring? I don't get it. All this time, just to get some tests done… How's that even possible?"*

Giuseppina had been moaning and nagging like a dripping faucet, so Luigi had to get in touch again somehow. The afflicted elderly mother had to chat with someone else who might tell her a few things, a few bits and pieces about her recovering son.

One of the same old stories from their scanty repertoire would have worked a treat. What mattered most was that their mum heard it from the lips of someone who represented an absolute novelty. A convincingly new narrator who would inspire her to hang on a little bit longer. A few more years. Until the Almighty would lift her out of that cock-sucking wheelchair that bled the three loving daughters dry twenty hours a day.

"Thing is... I've always been rubbish at telling fibs!" Nunzio sounded the retreat, as he began to sweat like a patrol in the midst of an ambush. With the three women controlling the circumference of the table as well as the perimeter of the dining room, which offered no escape route other than the internal balcony window.

"That's the thing. I've never been able to say something that wasn't true. From what I've gathered, your mum's brain is as sharp as a steel trap... I honestly don't think it would be a good move... I'm totally useless at it, you have to believe me! I really wish I could be of help, but... I'm truly sorry... Please forgive me!"

The three women had nonetheless anticipated the young man's conscientious reluctance. You needn't be very perceptive to figure how Nunzio was a nice fellow. The kind of person who will mull over things a billion times, before they even hint of either making a move or uttering a sound, with the noble intention of leaving everyone's feelings unhurt by their sage actions and words.

So they asked him again. But this time with extreme nonchalance. In such a suave manner that Nunzio stopped quaking in his boots.

As with the women's more recent and much more appeasing proposition, Nunzio would not have to come up with any material of sorts. Because Luigi's elder sisters were going to handle this extremely delicate aspect of the plan in person. The same way they'd had to personally handle Luigi's dirty behind when he was a baby, when the three sisters acted as his incumbent mothers. After all, the age gap was such that they'd been nominated the newborn's co-nannies.

Following the birth of her male son, Giuseppina's post-natal menopause had turned her conceited stride into a hideous hobble. With the booze ingested daily taking a further toll both on her fat arse and on her general parental alertness. Eventually she quit getting up altogether, without even bothering to go and check on her male heir. Who was left for ages on the potty, screaming in vain for his pie-eyed mum to go and wipe his paralysed buttocks.

But that was all water under the bridge. It no longer mattered if their mum had busted their balls, and if they had squandered their youth steering the house away from the rocks. Currently, the poor soul needed their support to cruise along until the Lord would get a bloody move on.

The three sisters were going to oversee the whole process, and in the meantime Nunzio should feel more than free to put his feet up. The information would be passed on to him orally or, should he wish to have something to fall back on, Patrizia would surely be more than happy to transcribe the whole thing – verbatim – on a piece of the best scrap paper they could find in the sideboard, thereby allowing the young soldier to go over his script at his leisure. Then, once inside their elderly mother's bedroom, he would simply say his lines.

Nice and clear, of course.

The part, they promised, would be extremely easy to learn – by heart. A few words he'd never be able to forget.

"But what if...?" hypothesised Nunzio, as he sought a reasonable excuse to flee the scene. "Imagine your mum asks me about something not mentioned on your bits of paper? Say, for instance, she wants to know the hospital's name... or the consultant's name... Imagine she asked me about the room and the ward where your brother is, or whether Luigi has lost any weight... What would I say then?"

"Well, if the worst comes to the worst... just make it up! Trust us, it'll be like a walk in the park!" Emilia reassured him.

"I do what? Like a walk in the park, you say?" yelped Nunzio.

"That's right, just make it up. No biggie!" screeched Patrizia.

Nunzio should have created what he didn't know out of thin air. As well as that, he was strictly expected to jot down everything he made up on the spot. As one of his impromptu digressions could have conflicted with the three sisters' overall plot, which, at a later time, may have proved tricky.

*

On being presented with the stage directions and the lines for the role, Nunzio took up the script at first sight. He read it in one breath, and the power of those promethean words engulfed him in a way that made the mnemonic aspect of the task unforced. Those were words which challenged the truth of death, and consequently death itself, along with its cynical maker.

Those seemingly banal words thought out by three upright women, who in their minds were only trying to protect their disabled mother's shabby heart, in reality disguised a subtle sentence, an indictment for Zeus and its impenitent fuck-up. Precisely. Zeus had screwed up and now Nunzio-Hercules was bound to rescue Prometheus and its liver from being sadistically nibbled.

The young shaven-headed soldier was going to teach that stupid moron a lesson he'd never forget.

God had it coming.

*

Last time you saw Luigi was a week ago. He had to get some X-rays done, but only as a precautionary measure. During the day, he just won't give in to the prospect of rotting in bed. He strolls around the ward chit-chatting with his comrades and fellow patients. He'll just have a word or two with those who flaunt their improved shape, perched like parrots on the windowsills scattered along the corridors. Whereas he'll spare no effort for the bed-constrained wretches, who are overjoyed every time they see the beckoning of his heart-warming smile.

He's a bit bored because he can't wait to get out of that place. So he can go home to his family, to his mum.

And that's pretty much it.

To pass the time he usually has a few games of cards with the lads. He's so talented at it, he's made a name for himself all round the ward.

Naturally, the food isn't that great. But it's not too bad either, considering the hundreds of invitingly hot meals that are served on time, three times a day.

He's fine. He isn't too skinny to the point of causing you apprehension. God, no!

For those who aren't used to having a bath, there are shower cubicles with plenty of hot running water; the nurses, who are themselves soldiers of clockwork precision, supply the towels and the bathrobes every morning at 07:00, along with the breakfast: croissants, jam & butter, orange juice, cappuccino... the whole shebang.

*

After selecting a fine-toothed comb from the bathroom cabinet, Vicenza marched towards the bedroom to accomplish her habitual *coiffeur* duties.

The door had been left ajar, which gave the inexperienced actor beyond the threshold a chance to take a cheeky peek. Through the crevice, Nunzio was able to lay his eyes on the lady to whom he had to lie. Crafted stories that, regrettably, wouldn't have altered the heart of the matter. No, he was going to have to tell that poor old woman a gargantuan load of crap.

The gold-lacquer pendulum of the clock went about its business, toiling away like an impassive loony.

However, since time had been sat on its arse in wait for her son's return, the old mother's hair, as white as the whites of her eyes, had stopped growing – just like that.

Upon unwrapping the hair bun from the back of her mother's head, Vicenza got the very same impression. But she kept this further piece of bad news to herself, for Giuseppina had always treasured her hair like a little schoolgirl. The elderly woman couldn't have cared less about her wrinkles and moles; not a bit was she annoyed by her crow's feet or by the lumpy varicose veins that looked like semi-shelled peapods. She wasn't fussed about her vanished molar teeth, which had put an end to her love affair with wood-fired sourdough bread.

Giuseppina didn't have a care in the world for any of her decaying body parts except her mane.

She looked truly happy, every time her eldest and most doting daughter told her that her hair looked as beautiful as ever. Vicenza would brush it gently, *so gently*, as though her mum were a tiny doll that, after a short and careful role-play, had to be reposed for more delight in the years to come.

Back in its tiny house with a clear view, since there were no silly windowpanes getting in the way.

Her mum was a little toy Vicenza could easily access to amuse herself, without the risk of being turned into the laughing-stock of her covetous younger sisters, who would both have jumped at the opportunity to ridicule their mum's primary carer.

*

As the hairdo was neatly finalised by the insertion of a *pettenessa*[1] – an Andalusian-style comb that infused Giuseppina with the melancholic stillness of a long-retired flamenco dancer – the three sisters got down to the job of getting their mum cleaned and ready for the challenging day ahead:

1. Patrizia extracted the commode pan and emptied its content in the loo.
2. Emilia wiped and soaped both the front and the back of her mum's lower body.
3. Vicenza washed and dried her with a towel, whose fringe undulated with her hectic inspection for any remaining damp spots.
4. The diaper was lowered, tugged and ultimately slipped on by the three women together, for no fewer than six well-trained hands and arms were required to heave up and hold their mum's plump body in position.

They told her about Nunzio after the arrhythmia medication, an asphyxiating sensation that clutched the old woman's oesophagus like wallpaper, despite her daughters' surgical precision in halving the capsule on the chopping board.

---

1   Neapolitan for **decorative** comb.

Giuseppina was forewarned about a young man who had come to bring her news of Luigi. But first she had to promise she would be behaving herself.

"His name's Nunzio."

"You've got to stay calm, though!"

"Or else we'll send him away, understood?"

"We don't want to see you getting too excited like the time when you got the phone call, okay?"

"Remember that?"

"Watch it, otherwise we'll see him out in a blink."

"Come on, be a good girl, will you?"

"Please, Mummy!"

And so Giuseppina tried really hard. As hard as her yielding soul could bear. She did her very best to please her preoccupied daughters. But, alas, as soon as she glimpsed the outline of a young man standing by her bedroom door, she just couldn't help it. She just couldn't, you know!

She couldn't help crying and crying.

The same outpouring of motherly love was shed upon her hearing *her son's voice* magically oozing out of the telephone.

Soon Giuseppina's bladder and bowels gave way as the rest of her body succumbed to the rapture; thawing and resolving into piss and shit that metamorphosised into the tributaries of a newly sprung hope. A maiden yearning flowing down her body, as it did on the night

Luigi was born. Amidst contraptions and malodorous fluids which sanctified every single vessel of her gestating organs up to the estuary of her anal sphincter.

Meanwhile, Nunzio was in no less state of trepidation. He got to the top end of the room and ensconced himself in the cane chair across from the elderly woman's shimmering eyes.

Both apparently circumspect, like two perfect strangers on a quaint train carriage. Two strangers who within an instant find themselves catapulted into the vast unknown of their fellow passenger.

Giuseppina hadn't forgotten her daughters' warning. Had she not been able to control herself, they would have got shot of the kid. And on that account she eventually succeeded in keeping her tears at bay.

She began by asking her son's comrade and presumably good friend whether he was from the local area. Was he married? Did he have an extended family with lots of brothers and sisters?

She went as far as inquiring about his father's age and whether he was still being employed by the army. Before she ardently sympathised with the young soldier's mother who, like all women whose men are away at the front, was the families' and the country's true lifeblood.

"It's hard going for a woman, son!"

*

Giuseppina was behaving impeccably. Would you not say? She never jumped down Nunzio's throat, nor did she subject him to a third degree. On the contrary, she took her heart on a few errands to distract it from her pounding fears. And only later, much later on, the elderly lady whose son had been blown apart by a grenade timidly asked the young soldier whether, by any chance, he had lately seen her son in the flesh.

VI

He had done alright.

Nunzio had scraped through, in spite of his self-confessed ineptitude into the realm of inventiveness. The only glitch, duly brought up during the three irate sisters' extensive feedback, was his blatant inability to watch his mouth.

"When someone is making up stuff like that, then they should at least make sure they can still remember it all five minutes later!"

Nunzio's excuse was undoubtedly lame. And his "I'm so sorry, I can't remember a single word of what I've just said to your mum" pissed the three women right off.

They were furious at him. Yet, on intuiting the young man's intention to take leave of their ungrateful responses, they kept their cool and had the foresight to write down his details lest he be needed again.

In order to eliminate the possibility of any transcription errors, Patrizia instructed the shaven-headed soldier to repeat his telephone number three times. Which he patiently agreed to do before haring off down the stairs.

The crossing of the open-air atrium offered him none of the solace he had been looking forward to. Nunzio pressed the chunky white button right next to the mosaic of multi-coloured letterboxes, then he casually saw himself out of the Lilliputian door.

But on passing the palazzo's threshold, Nunzio took very ill. As if the *train of daydreams* he had travelled on together with the elderly mother was presently careering down a track of its own. The train with the head in the cloud had really got carried away, entering a tunnel where the pitch-blackness assailed the conscript with a strangulating feeling of terror.

VII

It was scheduled for seven p.m., leaving no room for manoeuvre around the truth. The requiem mass for their brother and the rest of the soldiers from Company 51 was going to be held at such a late hour that their mum could not be fooled in any way. At seven o'clock without fail, the three sisters and their elderly mother convened in the dining room to discuss the meal to be cooked.

The vegetables were laid out on the table for the women to punctiliously inspect and evaluate their freshness. Though the final decision always rested with Giuseppina, the shaman-matriarch who fiddled with the peppers and what-not until she picked the one that deserved to make it into the pot or frying pan more than the rest.

On the evening of Luigi's memorial mass, in the same post where his company seemed to have put down roots, Nunzio was handed a blue-pencilled letter.

It was from Vicenza.

In a grandiloquent request adorned with an underlying insecurity and angst, the woman begged him to return, to have a chat with his mum, since she had repeatedly asked for him. They were aware that it might have been months before he could be granted a new leave of absence, however the three sisters promised that his second visit would also be the very last one. Then, if their mum asked to see that dear friend of her son's again, they would just tell her the army had transferred him to some faraway base where a return home would have been unfeasible.

Nunzio couldn't get his head around the letter's moral implications, although – deep down – he had already made his mind up. He trudged up to the telegraphist's tent and requested permission to send an important communication home.

Astonishing. Nunzio, who had always been a duffer at telling lies, conned the buck-toothed operator into believing that the message was destined for his own folks.

I SHALL BE THERE AS SOON AS I CAN

It was a rash move, but that was the only way to do it. Had he given the tiniest thought to the elderly woman's loss, to her gaping grief that would have been ultimately left untouched by his jolly stories, he would have felt the overpowering urge to put that stupidly stubborn letter in the bin. Right away.

I SHALL BE THERE AS SOON AS I CAN

In the end, despite all reservations, he would have done it. This way, he thought at the end of the day, his next 48-hour licence would have been put to a good use.

Not his own, nor the truth's.

His intervention would have answered a distress call from a family who risked being washed overboard, as a result of a self-orchestrated tempest.

Nunzio-Ariel had to sweep up after Prospero's mess. And so it happened, less than a month after his telegraphic promise, that at around two in the afternoon, the young soldier and actor, whose hair had grown a little since his debut, materialised himself on the white floor-tiled stage inside the elderly woman's bedchamber, with a pocketful of good news about her dead son.

Their second encounter and second journey together would be a different story, though. The two had already met and conversed intimately, making the use of salaams or any other affectation completely redundant. Also, Giuseppina had learnt the sound of his mellifluous voice, so much so that she would have recognised it among hundreds.

"It's me, open up!"

While Patrizia plodded away at cutting her nails, the old woman almost jumped at the sound of the visitor's growing impetuousness. The buzzer's faltering microphone had been in need of repair for some time, coercing the occasional visitor into an operatic stunt.

In an effort to avoid any possible offence, Nunzio candidly explained – again and again – that he was not being ceremonious. He simply didn't want any bloody coffee. So, without further ado, he told the three sisters there were still a few things that were left unsaid.

More precisely, as Nunzio was very keen to articulate, on his first visitation he had scarcely had a chance to tell their mum half of the things, half of the lines that the three women had written down for him, on a bit of scrap paper he had cherished ever since in his pulpy leather wallet.

"That's great. Listen, though..." warned the three sisters. "Should you inadvertently say something that doesn't appear in the part we've given you..."

"You just can't keep it to yourself!"

Honestly, you've got to let us know everything you've said to her..."

"Or else..."

"Or else the two versions of the facts won't match!"

"You don't know this, but our mum is still sharp as a tack!"

"She remembers everything, you see?"

It was true. For someone of her age, Giuseppina was mindful and observant in a way that was genuinely baffling. Like a hawk, she was able to detect any alteration to all matter and living things who inhabited her landscape. And, by the use of this same gift, she instantly spotted a change in Nunzio's appearance.

"That's a cute cut you've got there, son! That's good, the baldy style just didn't suit you. It kinda made you look like a convict: the ghost of the Count of Monte Cristo!" laughed Giuseppina heartily, with her toothless gums tenderly exposed like a smiling infant's.

Ten minutes went by, without the shadow of a reference to her son. The elderly mother appeared to be in an excellent mood and in much-improved shape. She stout-heartedly pushed on with her ad-lib performance by using anything that came on her radar at that point. Like her all-pervading hair, of course.

She patted it and stroked it cautiously as a veil of fleeting serenity reposed on her frown. Giuseppina had no idea why her hair had stopped growing. It felt like a million years had passed since her eldest daughter last positioned her wheelchair in the very centre of the room – right between the two mirrored wardrobe doors – so that she could assess the growth by seeing it for herself. Vicenza aligned her right leg against her mum's loosened hair, so that doubting Thomas could finally get a grip and see how her abundant fleece had gone well past her knee.

She just didn't know what was wrong with it, and why it wouldn't grow as much as it should. Maybe it was because of the odd mid-season weather, she thought. Or perhaps a consequence of her declining strength, the first signs of which had manifested after she stopped eating meat; irrespective of the time of day, Giuseppina's body seemed to have developed an intolerance to animal tissues that, when ignored, punished her with abdominal pain and a languor that could last for days.

*

And so, together again, they left – their glances lobbed over the horizon line. Chug after chug, the hot-headed train left the second-floor apartment bedroom taking Giuseppina and Nunzio on two very individual journeys by a much-shared destination.

The young soldier and the elderly woman sat quietly across from one another, burrowed away in the carriage that skipped through the concrete dark. They did not know where they were going and they couldn't have cared less to find out. All they wanted to do was make it to a place that came with some fleck of hope.

VIII

As far as Giuseppina *knew*, the tales told by Nunzio were the *holy truth*. And she held this very principle in a higher regard than any other. She *believed* them, and opened her heart to every word that fluttered about the young conscript's lips with the most spontaneous and disarming ingenuousness. For she could feel the *truth's* gentle touch on her barren skin. Those fibs gave her the proteins, the collagen that pasted every fragment of her being into one living form.

By and large, the three sisters' plan fared well. Their paralysed elderly mother had fallen for it completely. Moreover, her spirits seemed to be recovering thanks to the liniment injected in her veins through Nunzio's verbal drip. The women really sensed they were muddling along. Though soon enough Giuseppina's poor appetite became a new reason for concern. The ordinary feeding battles had evolved into a full-scale siege against the poor old woman, who would strenuously fend off all nourishment, while her mouth was barricaded against any medication that her pushy carers might have tried to jemmy past her lips.

It was in Nunzio's tales that the nutrients she truly needed were found. Nutrients that for the sweet old lady, completely nauseated by her son's "predicament", were as reinvigorating as a rib-eye steak – cooked on the grill as prescribed by the tradition that the three middle-aged women had strived to retain.

The sisters' induction went back to the happy days of their idyllic childhood, when their parents were not yet holding a grudge against them because of their failure to find a husband, one who would be appeased by their meagre dowries, and when their father was still managing to suppress his impulse to abandon the family, by distributing all his spare time between the wine shop next to the patisserie and the snooker club – venues strictly prohibited to moaning, whining or even remotely ranting females.

The little hair-plaited girls had to build up their knowledge by peeping through the interstices of the folding door, since their mum didn't want the abominable smell of charred meat from the small kitchen to mar their spotless Sunday dresses. They glimpsed the blood-dripping grill hover over the gory burner gas hob, and tried to learn as much as they could by committing it to photographic memory.

Still, after all these years, nothing had changed about the way the meat was served in their house: with a previously dressed salad on the side. Undeterred by their equally high cholesterol levels, the three women chomped on the bits of fat and slurped the blood that had subsided at the bottom of the plates.

They drank every droplet of blood even though it was revoltingly tepid. One of them gurgled, "The blood is truly the best part of a steak. It's fortifying. Come on, drink up... Don't you let it go cold!" while the other two remarked their agreement through an alternate succession of thrums and burbles.

The fortifying effect produced by the meat's blood could have equally allowed Giuseppina to carry on, to hang on during her son's eclipse, which represented a momentary lapse of reason on God's part.

God had to return her son to her by some means. Because if it's true that the Almighty is always in the right, then it follows that He could not possibly allow the death of a son prior to that of the mother who bore him. Otherwise it would mean that this bozo of a Creator doesn't have a frigging clue what He's doing. Moreover, if a tragedy of such unimaginable entity were possible, if kids could die before their mothers and fathers, it could only mean that God has lost His marbles.

Which would not compute in the slightest.

It wouldn't make any sense. And because of this you could no longer have any faith in Him. In such a God, one that has completely lost the plot, no-one could ever believe.

*

Since he had not been able to rely on any oral or written prompting from the three sisters, Nunzio was forced to take all story-telling matters into his own methodical hands, by musing on anything that might carry the signs of a cool tale. Which is precisely what happened in the early afternoon of the day when he returned to the second-floor apartment, at the exact time when the smell of grilled meat from the kitchenette had already saturated the adjacent dining room, and was now beginning to imbue the elderly lady's bedroom.

On recognising his jerky saunter through the rank mist, Giuseppina greeted the young conscript as joyfully as she had done on the first occasion.

"Hi, I'm so happy to see you! Come in, come in. Here, take a seat. How are you, son?"

When all of a sudden her face secreted a grimace of unsuppressable revulsion. A complete sense of sickness to the stomach which turned the old woman's glee on its head.

"The smell of roasting meat is so nice, I think," commented Nunzio who, notwithstanding his generally poor appetite, sternly contradicted the old woman waiting for her dead son. Before he boldly went on to tell her how "One night, it just so happened that your son saved my life. He saved my skin from being roasted to death!"

*

"One night..." commenced Nunzio, with the adroitness of the storyteller who has fully got the hang of his bull-shitting role, "After a trek of more than ten miles, scouring every clod in search of the enemy, our lieutenant thought it was too late to return to the camp. Benighted as we were, he figured it would be a lot safer to stay put until the morning.

One fourth of Company 51 would have quartered in that plot of land, right outside an apparently empty homestead that we were unable to reconnoitre, because the batteries in our flashlights were all dead.

Later on, round about eleven, when each one had already snuggled under the boughs in the nearby orchard, me and Luigi sneaked away and got in. We contravened our officer's orders and walked right through the farmers' house door, having cunningly eluded the not-so-watchful eye of Michele, a lad from

Lake Avernus[2] who would always volunteer for the first sentinel shift; he much preferred to sleep right through. "Right past the night!" is what you'd often hear Michele say.

With the exposed tuff masonry only faintly gilded by some slack moonlight, the two-floor dwelling had been lying vacant since the farm labourers hastily abandoned it, taking with them nothing else but the cause of their eviction, the pictures and portraits arrayed over the yellowed walls. The walls which, defaced, were left to shroud the reticulate niches of an above-ground catacomb.

Their breaching of the Ministry's ban on *commemoration tools* had cost that family their home as well as their livelihood.

Notwithstanding the heavy bombardments which frequently hoed that area until the last seed of terror had been sown, the recently puttied windowpanes didn't seem to have suffered the loss of a single fragment, while the rest of the ground floor lay bare, apart from a table and four chairs still snooped towards the dormant furnace.

---

2 A volcanic crater lake of major importance to the Romans, who considered it to be the entrance to Hades.

Shortly afterwards, as if he knew the place like the back of his hand, Luigi beckoned me over with a flick of his head, as he set foot on a stone staircase.

Upstairs, I distinctly remember, there were two bedrooms. One of which was barely more spacious than a deep closet. Whereas the master bedroom had in its centre a king-size bed that could have easily accomodated four adult bodies.

The big bed was made. As I crouched over the thick layer of dust, I was overwhelmed by a wonderful scent that rose up from the depths of the sheets; a lily petal scent, I thought. Though I wasn't sure, for I am no botanist, of course.

Out of the corner of my eye, next I see Luigi rummage through the dressing-table's bottom drawer. His search becomes progressively more frantic, and it's eventually abated only by a finding – in the soft folds that hid them from enemy eyes.

Soap bars.

Everyone knows how peasant women use them to protect the linen's freshness from the fetor of worm-eaten furniture.

In the collection found by Luigi there were all sorts and makes, with the price labels still standing high on each one. On all but one, in fairness. On the lily-scented soap bars there were no indications of their cost to be seen. Perhaps because to the toil-worn countrywoman they held a sentimental value. Or maybe she didn't want her controlling husband to find out what he would have pugnaciously disapproved of.

I have no idea, really.

Next thing I remember, your son and I are both lying down. Roosted on the edges of the bed, we have to be careful not to make any false moves; the wool-fitted mattress is basically a sinkhole, possibly caused by the monumental weight of the evicted ploughman, akin to Polyphemus both in size and mannerism.

Luigi is lying at the far end of the room, ten inches away from the window. A soap bar clutched in his hands as if he were devoutly holding onto a holy picture of Saint Rita of Cascia, yet another woman who suffered at the hands of an abusive husband.

It finally seemed like we were going to get a chance to give our shattered bones a little break. My sentinel shift was from two to four and I was much in need of a decent shut-eye. But at that very moment, despite having complained all day long about the interminable march across many a desolate plain, Luigi started to act like an insomniac who will find any pretext to keep everyone else around them awake.

Your son wanted to chat. That's right, he fancied a little gab. As if we were sitting at a table in a tavern, immersed in the bucolic setting of a pergola, and with our memory of the outside world cut off by the cascading vines.

It got to the crazy point when he was telling me a bunch of silly old jokes. I quickly lost my temper and told him to give me some peace. Since we were lying down with our backs turned to one another, I could not see his face. Yet I was able to feel – quite clearly – how he was sulking like a little boy. A little boy sorely disappointed by his pal who had refused to listen to his good old yadda yadda yadda.

In the meantime, tens of minutes had marched on.

As soon as his shift was done, Michele did not give a great deal of weight to the lieutenant's orders and decided to join us. He flumped in the middle of the bed, causing a ravine-like depression in the mattress.

Due to my extremely light sleep, the second Michele sank in the bed, I sprang up like a jack-in-the-box. Luigi and I were top while Michele was tail, his cranium squashed against the minimally carved headboard.

By this time your son is snoring away. And little does he know of our new sleeping companion.

I got up tens of times. I had set the alarm on my watch but I was still nervous; quite often I couldn't hear it even though it blared in my ear like a freaking mockingbird.

After an exhausting series of tosses and turns, I found the way to knock myself out. Just to be roused again, not more than five minutes later, by Luigi's balmy voice.

"Nunzio, wake up!"

That's all I heard him say…

Through the blackness, I gape at his shadow as it floats over the bed and glides toward the door. Luigi steps outside the room for a few seconds and then rushes back inside.

Next, all hell breaks loose.

Passing through the door gaps, a torrent of smoke began to submerge the bedroom, forcing us to run to the window ledge where we barely had the time to decide who was going to jump first, before the hot smoke and then the flames would char us alive.

Michele was first to clamber out; he held onto the sill, with his legs dangling through the air for a couple of seconds, before he let himself go. Then came my turn to take the plunge and lastly Luigi's, who was the only one not to suffer a single scratch or graze from the 10-foot drop. Michele and I had sprained our ankles pretty badly; we were groaning and whimpering like dogs, in fact; our eyes fixed to the ground where our limbs were temporarily shackled by the excruciating pain.

Oh, believe you me, signora Lopez: the pain was really awful!

We were safe, though. Luigi had saved our lives by simply waking us up from what would surely have been a horrendous death.

At this point we're all looking up, startled by the thick smoke spewing out of the bedroom we've just miraculously fled. The smoke, and then the fire. The same raging fire that the Ministry of Camorra pours into every soldier's heart – the glowing inferno that must lick up our hearts and minds to purportedly protect our nation from every evil – that stupid fire had nearly killed us.

Can you believe it?

The sight of the torched house gave both Michele and me an incomparable sense of relief. Though I was soon to be taken aback by Luigi's mournful frown – an insurgent dirge which soon contaminated our ease.

For he clearly knew; he already knew what had happened to the rest of our comrades.

Wasted. Every single one of them.

It must be that the lieutenant changed his mind, therefore granting permission to the soldiers camped in the orchard to go and find shelter inside. Where, by the power of human suggestion, they would have been a lot warmer by simply persuading themselves that the stove was alight and crackling away.

All our comrades from Company 51 wanted to do was catch a little heat, and instead they ended up treated as lumpwood. Burnt alive. Their faces charred like pigs on a spit. The same spit we all sat round the day before, that had caused every single one of us – famished soldiers on the prowl – a certain degree of sympathy towards that poor innocent creature of God.

You couldn't recognise their faces. You couldn't tell Antonio from Francesco anymore.

The slaughter-house had almost been swallowed up. A few yards away from its ruins we stood still, before the freezing night-air-ringed funeral pyre, until the last ember of life was turned to dust.

We waited for hours and hours, with our backs turned, not having the balls to look in our friends' bulging eyes.

It wasn't long before the day came upon us, yet we continued to wait, until the following night. We waited in the hope that the darkness might cloak the dead.

We stood there the whole time without proffering a word, like cursed cowards ashamed by our own survival. We didn't take a step, nor did we take a sip of water or any food. But, worst of all, none of us managed to squeeze out a bloody single tear.

It reeked to high heaven. That human carvery really stank. And within ourselves we already knew how it would have taken millennia to scrape it off the root of our souls. That goddamn stench, the stench of the worst death there could have ever been. Completely messed up in the mind of whoever wrote down our destiny for that night.

We waited until the last puff of smoke had dissolved in the gentlest of zephyrs. Then we began to recover the bodies of our comrades from the sea of ashes beneath our feet. One by one, we carried them towards the orchard. Michele and I couldn't stand the sight of the dead and kept our eyes well away, particularly from their fire-ravaged faces. Luigi, on the other hand, focused on moving all the corpses away from the rubble as quickly as possible. As if he were carrying injured soldiers on a stretcher, injured soldiers on their way to the medical tent who would later have been transported to the nearest military hospital. Your brave son could look at them in the eyes as though those poor dead kids had to be reassured. Because, despite their seared bodies, they would have made it, one hundred per cent.

The doctors would have fixed them up all right.

Outside what was once the homestead's front door we found the vast remains of Franco, who had taken over the sentinel's post after Michele. The guy was so massive compared to everyone else that we hardly had any doubt: it was Franco, a twenty-year-old well- built shepherd from the island of Ischia who had been butchered like a lamb.

They had scythed his throat before he could raise the alarm, while Franco's eyes were drawn amid a convulsive powerlessness, before the unfolding massacre of his fellow fighters.

They had all been killed in their sleep. Their breath slashed away before they could even begin to ponder whether a vivid nightmare had perhaps moved the goalpost a little bit too far. Sentenced to death by the stealthiest of all enemies, who covers its tracks by burning each murder scene to the ground.

We lifted and carried every single one of them under the red mulberry trees where, seeped in murk, the soil just seemed to lie there, idly.

After all that, we spent the rest of the night holding a wake and praying for our fallen buds. We prayed even though we couldn't remember half of the sacred words that the military chaplain had taught us a year before. When, in a couple of hours or so, Father Giovanni rattled through the cathechism and had us all confessed with the holy body of Christ stamped on our tongues. All this blessedness on the same train that was taking us where thousands of poor kids die for nothing. There where the Ministry of Camorra – may God one day sling a noose around its wicked neck – had us fight the worst of all godforsaken wars.

IX

She was no blood relation. Having said that, she'd heard some of her neighbours' comments on the lady from the second-floor apartment across the street, on that poor old woman who – you need to listen to this! – was waiting on her dead son to come back from the front.

Hence it was purely out of respect for an elderly person who was suffering, if one early evening she decided to go and pay her an unannounced visit. Her genuine humanity made tangible by a family pack of sugar and coffee, gift-wrapped and tightly rigged by a golden curled ribbon. In Naples, coffee and sugar are a traditional gift choice for various occasions, ranging from the end-of-year expression of gratitude toward a teacher, to the more practical support for a family on the verge of a debilitating wake. The latter being nonetheless a circumstance that would be denied to the mother who, unbeknownst to her, had tragically lost her son along with his funeral and requiem mass.

Emilia, Patrizia and Vicenza told their mum that signora Consiglia, the lady who lived in the two-bedroom flat on the first floor of the palazzo opposite to theirs, had just popped in to make her acquaintance.

"Mum, the woman and her daughter Maria are sitting in the dining room waiting to see if they can come in; they would just like to say hello. A good neighbour's gesture kind of thing, you know!"

As soon as the visitors got up to follow the three sisters' single file, the atmosphere became in turn more dense and more grave, giving signora Consiglia and her thirteen-year-old girl the impression of being two dinghies raised from a canal, before they would be borne downstream to the old woman's inlet and up to her cove, where the ancient mother ship was berthed on a rust-laden chair.

Along the crossing, the three sisters did their utmost to paint the best scenery they could offer all round.

Emilia released the second leaf that was normally tethered between the top and bottom door bolt. Patrizia switched on the twelve-bulb crystal chandelier that in an hour consummed – or so they feared – more electricity than they would have spent on food in a week. While Vicenza, as per her housekeeping abnegation, dedicated her last efforts to the removal of her mum's fingermarks.

Giuseppina had developed a growing attachment to the glass dome of the gold-lacquer clock. A proper compulsion or fixation, one might say. Every morning she licked and licked her fingertips until they got all pruney, and then she daubed the glass shield of the clock, causing the pendulum, along with time as a whole, to disappear behind the cocoon spun by her saliva.

Sad to say, Vicenza never contemplated the possibility of an archetypal value behind her mother's senile disgustingness, thus adding this further chore to her routine with no questions asked. After all, the wiping of her mum's fingermarks was merely an extra orbital motion; hardly a new revolution about her mum's fat face and ass that she would have happily completed regardless. For in that universe that God had shamelessly left upside down, her mum represented the only firm spot she could see for millions of light-years.

Signora Consiglia lowered herself into an embroidered chair and pulled her daughter to her side. Maria managed to let go of her mum's wrench, yet the five-foot teenager eventually agreed to sit on her scaffold knees.

Visibly hurt in her adolescent ego, the young woman in skinny jeans decided to regain control of the mother and baby game; she slithered one arm around her parent's exposed shoulders in a way that conveyed an unintended sleaziness. Maria blushed beyond purpleness.

As Patrizia excused herself to go and prepare the coffee, Giuseppina took a good look at both ladies: signora Consiglia, the fowl woman who seemed to live only for the cocks that flitted about her shoddy bed, and her pretty hen who at that focal moment had the audacity to speak her young mind.

"I wanna a cup of coffee too, by the way!"

"Shush! Please don't take notice of this cheeky lady here," scowled her mum. "She's still young, and I don't wan't her to get hooked on coffee yet. As if all her other bad habits weren't enough already! Will you please just give her a glass of tap water?"

Coincidentally, remarked Patrizia on her return from the kitchen one minute or so later, the tap water in their area was amongst the most salubrious in the whole of Naples, as it ran through the same pipes that supplied the nearby San Gennaro dei Poveri hospital. The three sisters were really convinced about the healing power of their house water, which they thought contained plenty of sulphur to complement or even surrogate the proteins found in meat. Emilia went as far as estimating that, in nourishment terms, a pint of water from their tap was roughly the equivalent of a chicken fillet nugget.

Clearly it was just another load of crap, nonetheless Maria put on her most polite face and swigged what her tastebuds could only tentatively identify as a rotten-egg slush. Immediately after that she was lured into a telepathic beckoning, a call from the elderly woman who had – of this she was positive – something crucially intimate to tell her, despite their being complete strangers.

Entranced, she got up from her mum's knees and moved right next to the old woman hung on the right armrest of her wheelchair.

"Come here, hen!" muttered Giuseppina persuasively. She then tugged at little Maria's blouse sleeve so that she would bend down more and more, to the exact point where the young girl's left ear was levelled at her lips. The grieving old woman proceeded to whisper something to her, something that must have sounded particularly shocking, for Maria let go of Giuseppina's hold and ran back to her mum's lap.

"Mum, do you not remember how rude it is to whisper into someone's ear in front of other people?" scolded Emilia. "Oh dear, dear! Look at this child's flustered little face!"

Signora Consiglia, who didn't love the truth any less, demanded to know every word her daughter had heard from the sick old woman, who remained self-absorbedly engaged in a tug of war with the unyielding ribbon of the wrapping paper – a useful household item she aimed to preserve for future use.

On hearing the truth from her daughter's trembling lips, signora Consiglia glared at the three sisters who were responsible for their incapacitated mother, and who were consequently also liable for her blabbering. Where else could the elderly woman have got such a mad idea from? If not from her three bitchy daughters?

"Your mum is a big whore. She lies in bed with three men at a time!"

This is the shocking accusation Giuseppina had whispered into young Maria's dumbfounded ears.

It was time they got up and left before things got out of hand. Signora Consiglia held out her right arm before young Maria latched on with her left one, like a two-ring mother-and-daughter chain, a defensive formation that would protect them against any further attacks they may have suffered along the way to the front door and down the stairs.

"We'll see you later, signora Lopez!" shouted signora Consiglia, looking daggers. "And take care of yourself!"

As they set foot on the first stair, they let the heels of their shoes sound the war drum as loud as they could. But their anger prevented them from keeping a synchronised beat, which caused the glove maker Ciro Maresca to waken from his somnambulant hammering away at the sewing machine. The *guantaro's*[3] workshop was a vastly unauthorised makeshift box plastered around the void of the stairwell on the second floor. A birdcage that had cunningly occupied the irresistibly empty space left by the lift that the short-sighted owners of the rest of the apartments in the palazzo had always refused to invest in.

---

3   Neapolitan for glove maker.

The solitary man, hunchbacked by his art's inclination for seamless labour, took too long to rouse his legs and feet from the torturous crampedness. So by the time he got out he missed them. His eyes did not capture a single frame of the banging heels that sounded like two gigantic castanets. All he could see in the distance of the atrium were two eels scampering out of the portal, which they also forgot to shut.

Completely unaware of the content of their mum's libellous whispers, Emilia, Patrizia and Vicenza rushed to the gallery but did not make it in time to say *arrivederci* to them. "Mamma mia!" they thought – they really had to be in some serious rush to leave in such an uncivil haste.

"Grazie Don Ciro!"

They had literally run away like mad, their view being shared by the glove maker who from the first floor landing had to send his words flying to the three women skewered on the veranda upstairs: *"Prego Signo', prego!"* [4]

*

Through the slim portion of panes that the shutters seemed unwilling to cover in full, Giuseppina glanced at signora Consiglia and her little girl hopping on the

---

4 "You're very welcome, ma'am."

pavement across the street, before they bowed their heads under the portal of their own palazzo, whence they vanished in a wink. Then, in that very same spot, less than an hour later the elderly woman noticed a swanky car with its hazard lights on. The engine of the metallic painted car had possibly been turned off, nevertheless the sinister-looking automobile looked as though it were secretly whinnying like a thoroughbred horse demanding entrance to the castle for its high-born knight. Signora Consiglia's ex-husband had come to pick up his girl, for his fortnightly stint of paternity had been overdue for some time now.

Whenever she spent time with her father the young girl felt a lot more like a woman, and the first thing she requested from her ever-spoiling *babbo*[5] was that the two of them go for something to drink in some classy bar with a romantic sea view, a place where they would have been able to hang out in private – just the two of them.

From her bedroom balcony, signora Consiglia watched her treacherous daughter get in her substantive father's car. Not once – for Christ's sake – did that little ingrate lift her head to pay some sort of obeisance, or perhaps to tell her mum that she would give her a ring later on, or anything like that.

---

5   Italian for daddy.

It was just that the young lady was presently too busy to acknowledge her mum's affection deficit disorder. One single eye-contact and she would have given her the selfish list of all of the things that only mattered to her: starting with the precept of unrelented vigilance at all times, followed by the veto on any unsupervised promenading around her dad's estate, which was crawling with rednecks and mobster-wannabees.

But signora Consiglia had to be completely out of her mind, if she really thought a thirteen-year-old girl like her daughter might go for a mosey with her dad breathing down her neck like a trooper.

Needless to say, he took her to an extortionate terraced cafeteria for a milkshake, where the breathtaking view of the bay apparently made the self-tormenting patrons privy to the latest in panoramic simony. Then, shortly after they had returned to the suburban wasteland, Maria changed into a more flirtatious attire, a *femme fatale* outfit that her mum would have never approved. She touched up her make-up, raising its brilliance to dazzling point, applying an extra coating of lipstick, so that on her way out she could imprint it on her dad's right cheek. That way, after being bamboozled in his male ego, he would never have said no to her. He would have let his only daughter go out with her girlfriends, who would have all complimented her on her stunning figure, alongside the silver-hooped earrings whose low-frequency chiming would have whipped up instant enchantment.

They asked her where she had bought them but her reply was nothing more than a timid shrug of her shoulders. She hadn't the faintest idea about the shop's name or of their cost, since they had simply come out of one of her mum's dressing table drawers.

Maria had grown into a beautiful young woman, who would bring tears to her mother's loving and proud eyes every time she gazed at her transformed little girl reflected in the mirror. She was only thirteen, and surely signora Consiglia wasn't expecting her daughter to wear them any time soon. Yes, they were hers, hers to keep. Though, for the time being at least, only to be kept in a padded box together with the rest of the jewellery, the costly presents she received on the day of her first holy communion.

Maria was far too young to resemble a seductress.

Outside her dad's estate, the congregated boys waited a long time to witness her splendour, at a moment in the early spring evening when – they knew this would happen – the green warmth would lead to the discovery of a new region in her uncharted teenage body.

Clinging to one another's arms like daisy chains, normally girls of her age would walk up and down the main street in open defiance of their parents' modesty, while the boys on their squawking mopeds soared past them like geese in the last days of the mating season.

Though on that very night signora Consiglia's daughter decided to fly solo. Due to Maria being a "barbarian" from the city centre, the girls often boasted their tacky turfdom by making her feel uncomfortable, and most importantly unwanted. So on that Saturday night the young lady went out by herself, swaying down the road and feeling as if the eyes of every single boy in the world were on her – longing for her.

The hoop earrings rocked back and forth in a seemingly fruitless stir, until Maria brought their oscillation under control between two of her fingertips; she would complete this operation at a junction or when she found herself on a stretch of pavement that was too dimly lit. Then the earrings turned into the faithful compass that would lead her back to the boys' warming flattery.

Hours passed, and the night's finale did not even come close to the one she had envisaged. Not a single boy approached her with some silly chat-up line that she might have shared with her girlfriends, before they would have all laughed their heads off at the boys' desperate attempts to impress her.

Without ever intruding, the geese got off their mopeds and alighted the pavement, from where they began to shadow her through the town. They went after her as though Maria were a sacred cow whom they could only check out from a respectable distance. The boys followed signora Consiglia's young lady in some sort of up-her-ass procession, like three pilgrims who, in the maiden girl's holy footsteps, seemed to have finally found their way.

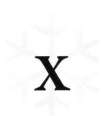

X

Based on the oath made by the three sisters, who couldn't exactly claim to be women of their word, Nunzio's second visit was due to be his very last show. Their brother's comrade would have delivered the performance of a lifetime at their mum's bedside stage; an apotheosis of fibs – a sleight of hand that could have earned it the title of *deception master class.*

But then, of course, things went very differently. The young conscript ended up spending most of his furloughs next to the anxious elderly woman waiting for her departed son. He even turned up a few days before Christmas to voice Luigi's personal season's greetings.

In his own words, the boy was extremely upset as it had been a good while since he'd had a chance to give his mum another call. The problem was, as Nunzio in his initial role of chorus began to preamble, the military hospital had seen the arrival of a new director who was an absolute pain in the neck. Professor Grimaldi was determined to assert himself in his new tenure by means of a "revolutionary therapy" that had to be accepted by all patients, especially the younger ones:

ALL CARD GAMES ARE BANNED
WITH IMMEDIATE EFFECT

Grimaldi was of the view that hospitals were no place for chance and gambling. Hence no one, and particularly the patients who had already recovered the use of their legs, should be allowed to touch another deck of cards or even to dream of playing another single game. Besides, none of them could afford to play for real – with money to bet, that is – their miserable wages being just enough to keep their families off the streets.

The soldiers' need to play seemed nonetheless an unstoppable drive, much stronger than their need to win the war. After all, who were they really fighting against, and what were they fighting for? Peace? Security? Prosperity? Social justice? Not a chance. Even the greenest recruits knew damn well that this was all about the Ministry of Camorra. It was all about the cronies that had run it for centuries, alongside the hereditary pups born from the Gattopardo's ever-broody loins.

While the injured soldiers saw the games as a small window-opportunity for their individual talents to shine, the new director, on the other hand, was not the type to appreciate any larks, nor was he the fella you'd be wanting to trifle with. So much so that on the second night after his arrival he instructed all medical staff to rake through every aisle of the hospital. They were given carte blanche, including the right to search and frisk the patients; if they caught someone playing in the toilets or in the prayer room, they were authorised to restrain the perpetrators and strip the cards away from them, one by one.

It was for the soldiers' own good.

"You'll see how they'll get the message," Grimaldi reassured his henchmen.

Despite a few subversive players, who were adamant about pushing their luck beyond the long and hairy arms of the law enforcers, the new director's plan seemed to have taken off. All was well until the early afternoon, when Luigi and three of his fellow die-hard comrades turned up outside Grimaldi's office. They had momentarily surrendered their cards.

Nevertheless, they hadn't given up all hope on the idea, on the concept of playing and the libertarian principle that underpinned their games.

They kept their hands tucked in their half-ripped pyjama pockets, and they formally introduced themselves as the leaders of the CPS – a newly-formed union that represented the rights of all Card Playing Soldiers. After that, they put their offer on the director's table, a goodwill gesture that had allegedly received the backing of all their members.

They solemnly promised to cast all gambling to one side, for good. In return, the director would recognise the soldiers' right to play for amusement purposes, especially in consideration of the fact that every hour spent inside the wards felt a lot more burdensome than the actual seriousness of their wounds and conditions.

Just to kill some of the time they had on their hands.

"But none of this *time on your hands* is really *yours*, is it?" rebuked the professor dourly. Before he surprised himself with a counter-proposal that in his view might have cajoled the Ministry of Camorra into granting him early retirement.

The head physician's offer to the impudent handful led by Luigi, who valiantly stood one pace ahead of the other three, was completely unexpected, and caused a minute or so of speechlessness in the caucus.

"Ok guys. What more can I say? You win. From this instant, the ban on card games is lifted. But on one condition, mind. You may only play a game where the ultimate aim is losing. I personally recommend the *Chi perde*.[6] Just to let you know, this sort of practice has been popular across Europe for centuries. In England they called it *Losing lodam*,[7] whereas in Spain it was rebranded

---

6 'Losing' – a reverse card game where the main aim is to throw penalty cards on a trick won by somebody else.
7 A distant relative of today's 'Hearts'.

Gana pierde and in France *Qui gaigne perd*. Though the ultimate goal remains always the same: winning by scoring the lowest possible number of points."

*

To round off his tale, Nunzio told Giuseppina how Professor Grimaldi was soon nicknamed *Ace of Clubs*, the card that was now worth 11 penalty points and that was feared more than the last rites. Then, he manifested his disapprobation for the card-playing soldiers all around the hospital, who didn't take very long to acclimatise to the new rules.

"Not my Luigi, I hope!" erupted the elderly mother. "Surely, my son is a fighter, and not a happy loser."

In response to her deep concern, Nunzio hastily confirmed Giuseppina's expectations and concluded his act by telling her all about the time when her son realised the rub therein. For in the losing game imposed by *Ace of Clubs* lay a profound humiliation of the players' talent and dignity, one that in the long run would have made cowardly shits of them all.

XI

For the three sisters, telegrams, letters and hand-delivered messages were no longer required. On his own initiative, Nunzio would go and see their mum at least once a month, turning up at her bedside with a previously unreleased story, a pristine account he had to tell straightaway before it slipped out of his mind. Partly harrowing and partly gloomy, the young conscript's stories never failed to deliver on their promise, their commitment to soothe the elderly lady to her heart's content.

Throughout the day, Giuseppina would get herself worked up. She mulled over every possible mishap that might have got in Luigi's way back home. For hours on end, and then for days on end, she would be worried sick. She really could not believe that a new spring might see the light of day without her son returning home first.

Inside the dimly lit chamber, Nunzio and Giuseppina kept exclusively to themselves. Furthermore, they seemed to speak a different language altogether. A language of their own that remained incomprehensible to the three sisters, who would systematically eavesdrop, hoping to catch the gist of their murmured conversation.

Along with their tales, many a month passed.

Like intrepid swallows, years flew by the window of the dreamy train, where the improbable pair sat in a state of veritable collectedness: the young conscript who looked younger than ever, and, before him, the elderly woman whose buckled countenance now revealed her age, as well as the agony of her son's long-awaited return from the dead.

As per Vicenza's proclivity, Giuseppina was preened to perfection. Through the reflection in the mirror, her hair bun appeared as a crown of light, like the halo over a saint's head. A creature beatified prior to her natural passing because of the inhuman pain she would have to endure until her last hour. A saint who died from the complications of her unbearable grief. The grief that the anxious mother felt flowing through her veins, and that often caused her seizures; she levitated over her bed and chair as quietly as Saint Lawrence twitched on the gridiron.

Springtimes came and went until the fifth month of May landed on the old woman's doorstep. A stockpile of time, without any tangible sign of Luigi to be sensed anywhere around her.

On that lonesome stretch of road, and along the one-way journey that would take her right into the truth's womb, Giuseppina had become increasingly laconic. She sat as taciturn as the church bells in the piazza, whose knelling had been muted by thunderous war drums – a tannoyed call to arms from the sanguinary Ministry of Camorra.

At this point in her tantalising wait for her son, the pathos experienced by the elderly mother had dragged her frail body up to the eleventh station of the cross, where the soft tissues in her body had started to be undone by time and gravity together.

She was being flaked alive.

Giuseppina was indeed aware of Luigi's improving health, Nunzio never failing to provide her with largely reassuring bulletins. Still, the mere fact of remaing torn apart – mother and son – had evolved into a much more doleful circumstance than the mother's concern for her boy's life per se.

Caught up in his fib-telling galore, Nunzio had no inkling of the old woman's declining health, whose heart and mind were being demolished by the wrecking ball thrust by the gold-lacquer pendulum of the clock. Giuseppina's Alzheimer's disease had already been diagnosed for two years, despite the three sisters' desperate attempts to throw this medical opinion right back at the demented doctor – the bloodsucker who demanded they fork out for their mother's visit upfront. Nunzio was eventually informed by Emilia, who briefed him about the heart-wrenching news. One that had caused Vicenza and Patrizia a shock so vast that the two women were physically unable to tolerate the vaguest reference being made to *it*.

It happened one morning a few months back. Patrizia and Vicenza entered their mother's room holding the fresh water and the coffee in their heedful hands.

"O Lord, who's there? Who are you two? What are you doing in my house?"

None of the two middle-aged babies were remotely recognised by the elderly mother, causing the emergence of a sudden and premature distress. The women's knees shaking and ready to snap as though their adored parent had died at that very moment, at the same moment when her brain had packed in.

As Giuseppina's mental illness got out of hand, the three sisters sought out the priest's help. They strongly wanted a man of the cloth to assess their mum's latest nightmare, an absolute opprobrium where the poor sick woman had supposedly witnessed a romantic encounter between the Holy Virgin and three men; the mother of Jesus – go figure! – had been caught in bed with three male patients from the same ward as Luigi's.

"That big lying whore!" was Giuseppina's only comment.

In the old woman's evidently derailed dream, the Madonna still had that little tear stamped on her face. Albeit, contrary to all previous encounters, on this very occasion it was clear to see – plain as the nose on your face.

It was fake.

A phoney little tear, painted over her cheekbone so that her weeping would appear as one thing with the rest of the flesh underneath – the tissues of her body that gave her form and leverage.

"Her complexion was very dark. As dark as the Black Madonna I once saw at the Sanctuary of Montevergine. And, hear me out, she was lying in bed with three men!"

Giuseppina's recollection was thorough and vivid. Moreover, she did not omit the description of the three hugging men, who wriggled and quivered in the presence of the Madonna. They were going to stick with the lady, for there was no good enough reason to do otherwise. The three young soldiers held the Holy Virgin tight and marked her words while she, bawdier than any man, was at the dirtiest tricks of her carnal vocation.

She kept her voice down by moderating her *ad libitum* singing to a whisper, so that the other patients in the room wouldn't be roused. Though soon her *afflatus* was transmuted into the faintest and most melancholic of chants. A forlorn and poignant song. For the Holy Virgin, just like Giuseppina, couldn't find peace. Because of the distance. The void left by her sweet little son was pulling every atom of her being asunder.

The Madonna too was being flaked alive.

XII

The minute he fully gauged the desecration of the old woman's dream, Father Guglielmo cut all circumventions and headed straight for the harshest road ahead. The alleys all around the Rione Sanità had not long been bedewed by the fishmongers, who increased the appeal of their produce, along with the clams' urination, by splashing bucketfuls of sea water on their displays.

It was very early in the morning and Vicenza, Patrizia and Emilia had yet to get dressed. On the back of three chairs in the dining room, their folded petticoats and tights waited in line like the impatient parts of an unassembled suit of armor.

In the priest's humble opinion, their mum had to be put in the expert hands of an institution, where esteemed geriatricians would have the best chance to look after her specific needs. There was no denying that Giuseppina's condition had degenerated, possibly beyond God's reach too.

"He's in the wrong. He's in the wrong, goddamn it!" Giuseppina began her incensed *j'accuse*, with a calmness and lucidity of mind that left Father Guglielmo dumbstruck.

"He's in the wrong. The cock sings many a laud to the dawn, while the nightingale sits tight until the last lights of day have gone out. There's supposed to be a system, a one-way system whereby the players enter and leave the stage in the right order. Otherwise no story will ever make sense. It won't make any bloody sense anymore!"

"What is it that doesn't make sense, sweetie?" asked her Vicenza. "Come on, mum, let's go."

"Please, ma'am!" beseeched Giuseppina, as if her eldest daughter were merely a stranger. "Please, don't take me away from the window! Leave me where I can look forward to Nunzio coming to see me again. Please, ma'am!"

"God's sake, Mummy, stop calling me ma'am... It's me, Vicenza, the first kid you've ever had. Come on, come with me in the dining room. Emilia's making you something that, I swear, it'll make your mouth water."

"Emilia, you say, ma'am?"

"Stop kidding on, Mummy! Emilia's your youngest daughter. Remember, you named her after your little sister, the one that died at birth?"

"Youngest daughter? Daughters, you say? I have no daughters, ma'am!" claimed Giuseppina. I have a son, I have a baby son. Never had any girls, even though I would have liked one or two."

"Mum, you have three daughters and a son."

"No way. I have a son, I only ever had a son. Yes, it was the lady. It was the Holy Virgin who let me have him. 'Cause I made a vow to her, you see?"

"So, wh-wh-what are you saying, you want to disown the rest of your ch-ch-children now, eh?" stammered Vicenza, her eyes strewn with tears as bulbous as garlic beads.

"Ma'am, as I've already told you, I only have a son, by mercy of the Lady who shed her boundless grace on me. Besides, I couldn't have possibly borne any baby girls, since females give birth to themselves. Everyone knows that."

After taking the first sip of coffee, Father Guglielmo's gesticulating hands took centre stage on the dining room table, as he once again illustrated the possibility of a geriatric sanatorium, a prospect the three sisters had to ponder carefully and without allowing their filial emotions to tamper with the prime objective of doing the best for their ailing parent. The medical institution he was referring to was a centre of world excellence.

"Believe you me. We're talking about a place where beds are assigned as though they were lottery tickets!" exaggerated the priest without any misgivings.

Having predicted the moment when the three sisters would have found themselves in a dead end, Father Guglielmo had been making a few calls as well.

"I'm telling you, your mum would get a bed in minutes!" promised the well-connected churchman. "The minute I pick up the phone..."

The three daughters, more close-knit than ever, saw Father Guglielmo out while trying to demonstrate their appreciation for his unsolicited efforts.

It was never going to happen, though.

There was no way they would have dumped their mum in a luxury nursing home, because the love and warmth of your own home, they were sure, is something no-one could ever vaguely reproduce. Nobody was going to lay a finger on their mum but those three alone. Except, of course, for God, who was due to tow their mum's ass up to the heavens.

After they had sacrificed their entire lives around their mother's need for constant care, now the Lord – the bastard who had screwed them over for years – had to accept full responsibility for another one of his distressed children.

It had become very much a matter of principle. From that old apartment on the second floor of a historic palazzo without a lift, they were not going to take any shit from any nurses or doctors.

"God forbid!" appealed the three women in unison, merging their lamenting voices in the initial verse of a new prayer for all tormented souls.

*

For the sin committed by the mother in her possessed dream, Father Guglielmo was not in any position to tell the three hard-headed sisters whether an absolution would be possible. Again, he had to resort to one of his connections, this time at the diocese, where, disappointingly, they were unable to provide an exhaustive answer on the singular case.

It appeared to be a *quaestio* that, according to the bishop's secretary in person, could only be resolved by consulting the highest spheres in the Vatican.

XIII

On the Maunday Thursday, Nunzio clearly took his time. He apologised to Vicenza for the late hour, but "I really didn't want to leave your mum hanging!" avowed the young conscript.

He was right. If he'd missed a single appointment, Giuseppina would have been left suspended in a sleepless vacuum. She would have stayed up all night waiting on her son's comrade to come and keep his promise of eternal returns.

Nunzio had to bear a new story to the mother who lay in wait for a new series of events. A new plot that, alongside a garnish of fulsome anecdotes, would have kept Giuseppina's heart going, or functioning as she preferred to say: "I can't function without Nunzio, I just can't!"

As soon as her son's friend made it by her side, the elderly woman felt immediately relieved, and slightly hungry too. She didn't give her usual shake of the head, and received the plate that was presented to her with a glowing smile. The *migliaccielle*[8] had been lying in the dining room since lunchtime, guarded by Vicenza and Patrizia who had scrambled all enemy flies with dish-towel strikes of surgical precision.

In response to Emilia's battery of offerings, Nunzio, who had opted for an early dinner, courteously refused to sample even one single mouthful. Giuseppina gingerly observed the constistency of the fritters that, in her glimmering childhood memories, had to reach absolute compactness, so as to properly exalt the richness of the pork and cheese-based filling.

"They're totally firm, mum. I promise they are!" swore Patrizia with the dish towel loosely hung on her breastbone.

It was honestly mad; the sick old parent could no longer recognise her own daughters, neither their names nor their faces. Like unflappable moons, Vincenza, Patrizia and Emilia had clung on to their mum ever since the Big Bang of Luigi's death. But even so Giuseppina didn't seem to hold them dear anymore.

Like three chamberlains, for months they had been spelling out one another's presence and name before setting foot inside their lady's bedchamber. All for nothing, for Alzheimer's had already plundered their mother's memories, along with a huge chunk of the three

---

8   Traditional Neapolitan polenta fritters.

sisters' identity. Everything seemed to have been wiped out, gone.

And yet that shit-eating old cow was still able to recall the minutiae of her gastronomical preferences.

"The dough's too chewy... The sauce is too runny... This mozzarella's soggier than my tits... These cockles are defrosted shit!"

Giuseppina communicated her willingness to ingest a few bites of her meals by means of two antithetic facial expressions. Demeaning curled lip stood for "You can take this slop back to where it came from", whereas the condescending jutting out of her chin meant "Alright, I'll give it a go; it may well be not entirely vomitous!"

Contrary to the long-established norm, by the way she was opening her mouth nice and wide, and through her swallowing one morsel after another with a distinctive celerity, on this very night the three sisters were more than pleased to verify their mother's approval: the dainty they had spent hours making was to her liking.

Giuseppina honestly found the *migliaccielle* exquisite. She exerted her left arm and managed to raise it four inches or so. She then aligned the index and the middle finger of her suddenly tremorless hand, to complete the unequivocal request for "a sip of wine". Washing down the tanginess and pungency of the polenta would have been the bees' knees. A relish to die for.

*

Once more, by the window of a carriage they had all to themselves, Giuseppina and Nunzio delved into the obscurity beyond the panes. On the train that just couldn't sit still for the next journey.

XIV

While new springs kept coming and circling around the decrepit block, signora Consiglia remained in the same old carousel of unrequited and forbidden love songs. She had an anthology of all-time favourites, even though Sergio Bruni's sylvan vibrato, rather than any other interpreter's style and technique, seemed to be what sent a shiver down her spine.

Quite often she appeared to be listening to the same verses, until the words had conquered every nerve cell in her body. Those same lines that perhaps, from the muting distance of her bedroom, Giuseppina Lopez had come to crave even more than the return of her son Luigi.

The sick old mother from across the street wished she could hear what those morose songs had to say, and why they meant so much to the lady, the woman who had been left by her philandering husband to raise a family on her own.

Giuseppina would have loved to hear those lily-petal-scented words. So she tried to focus on the woman's lips alone, in the hope of capturing a syllable or two.

But, to her great disappointment, her attempt coincided with the pandemonium sparked off by the shopkeepers, who, in short succession, pulled their shutters down with a wrathful clangour.

The first-floor flat was wrapped in darkness, apart from two very small beacons on the sides of the lady's pretty face. Consiglia? Cybele? The Woman of Çatalhöyük? Theotokos? She was definitely a queen, a matriarch and a demiurge too. Still, beyond all appellations of sorts, what was the name that best represented her being an unmoved mover?

Signora Consiglia crept inside her daughter's room and looked through little Maria's jewellery box. She knew where to look and it did not take her long to find it, the jewellery box with the silver hoop earrings she had missed like a totem. She just wanted to try them on, feel them on for a few seconds and then, pinkie promise, she would put them right back. However, as she looked at herself in the mirror and realised how wonderful she appeared – as though she were pregnant again – she decided to keep them on a little while longer.

She had indeed passed them on to her daughter but she still had the bloody right to remind herself of her charm. The irresistible allure of the forty-something woman that she was.

She undid her ponytail and brushed her fringe down, until a French-style bob drew the teaser of a stage curtain over her forehead. It was show-time again, time she got in bed with the latest trio of men, who gracefully caressed her body while she twiddled with the silver hoops; her index and middle finger ran over the rim like the pulleys of a tread-wheel crane.

She needed her spirit lifted away from the misery of being on her own.

Jesus, that was really it. Amidst the tenebrae of her galloping dementia, in that moment Giuseppina saw all her delusions, the depression and paranoia that had led her to turn a good woman and neighbour into some slut.

In a definitive epiphany, the elderly mother recognised all the faces and names without a moment of hesitation or doubt. As if her worn-out brain had been granted a very last chance to return to its minted condition.

From the turret of her wheelchair, the old woman clearly saw the three men in her neighbour's bed and this time they were no longer faceless strangers or acquaintances. Her father Gennaro and her husband Alfonso were top, whereas her son Luigi was tail. The three men who, one after the other, had left her, dumping her with the part of the self-reliant amazon she did not have the strength or will to play.

1. Giuseppina was a little bit older than two when her dad Gennaro took off and migrated to the

States to become a crook with a passion for the young waitresses employed in his pizzerias.

2. Giuseppina had just turned forty when her husband Alfonso left her along with their four children, new-born heir included, to move in with a woman who was the same age as his youngest daughter.

3. Giuseppina was only sixty-five when her only son Luigi decided to join the army and follow his grandad's and father's presumed footsteps.

When the twelve-year-old Giuseppina eventually mustered the strength to inquire "Mum, why isn't daddy coming back?", the then chubby little girl was told that her *papà* had died in battle, and that she had to remember him as a man of great prowess.

The same 'prowess' load of shit that years later, time and time again, Giuseppina would use herself with her children, who remained secretly unpersuaded nonetheless.

Across seventy-five years and seven months of her life, they had all let her down. Father, son, and that ass-Holy Spirit that was her husband Alfonso. They had all dumped her.

"They've all forsaken me. Cunts." grumbled Giuseppina, after seeing the whole and naked truth for the very first and last time.

XV

At the military hospital, where Luigi was undergoing the new therapies enforced by the new Director *Ace of Clubs*, there was also a secluded ward for the *phthisics*, the tuberculosis patients who lay in a horrendous state of ill-health and neglect.

This was the prologue to a new chapter in Luigi's misadventures that Nunzio cared to share with an estranged Giuseppina, on an early summer morning, three months since their last sit-down together.

Before he continued, the young conscript quickly made all the necessary reassurances.

"Yes, it's true, TB is highly contagious."

However, the Alzheimer's-ridden mother had nothing to worry about, for her son's ward H was practically miles away from the dump for the *phthisics* that was the beleaguered ward P. Between Luigi and those lethal germs there were something like thirty ramps of dizzying stairs. Plus, a string of corridors and wide open windows that guaranteed a more than adequate ventilation.

The coughing and spluttering soldiers, whose consumption had been caused by the foulness of the war engineered by the Ministry of Camorra, had been relegated to the tenth floor of the sanatorium. The medical staff would access ward P through the main lift which was operated by a key, a release key that vanished into thin air every time the same lift was required to transport a phthisical patient.

At a recent staff meeting, duly attended by all medical and clerical employees, Professor Grimaldi had made it very clear to everyone:

- "I don't care if they are in a more or less serious condition, I don't care whether they need an urgent blood transfusion or an operation, the phthisics are not to get in the main lift.
- They are to be loaded on the freight elevator.
- And if anyone were to ever ask or complain, the release key has gone missing and we are awaiting a replacement from the central maintenance office in Rome."

In all honesty, Ace of Clubs had merely implemented an order that arrived by fax from the Ministry's central office. An executive order that Grimaldi read while glancing at an empty mahogany picture frame where, before the ban on commemoration tools, he used to keep a photograph of his wife and children.

No-one dared say a word to challenge the maltreatment of the phthisics, who were rammed into the same trash can that was used by the cleaners – a pestilent rat trap saturated with the noxious exhalations of chemical waste.

The Ministry of Camorra intended to hide the sight and thought of death – the man-made termination of life caused by its mindless war. It aimed to isolate all potentially terminal cases to protect the recovering soldiers' morale.

*

"Now. You know what your son is like, right?"

Giuseppina had clearly got off the train of drifting thoughts. Consequently, Nunzio diverted his story straight onto the track that led to the hero's intervention, the hero who will right any wrong by and by. The young conscript-playwright activated the *deus ex machina* who would have shown Professor Grimaldi who the daddy really was.

By coming in contact with the contaminated air of the freight elevator, the failing lungs of the phthisics were literally receiving the kiss of death. Therefore Luigi had to act quickly, as quickly as it was humanly possible, in fact.

XVI

Since their mum had forgotten all about them, the three sisters felt they had to wrap up everything pronto. Giuseppina was very much not herself anymore and this meant that their period of mourning could no longer wait. Well ahead of her physical death, they were due to grieve for the loss of the woman and mother whom they had tirelessly cared for throughout their lives.

Now, more than ever, Vicenza, Patrizia and Emilia needed God to rest their mum's crumbling mind. The whole thing needed to be wrapped up, including Nunzio's tales. It was time the word of God took the floor now, so that their mum could bow out with dignity and her soul still remain in one piece.

On the night of his last appearance, Nunzio arrived even earlier than usual. At the front door, he was brusquely asked by Patrizia to hand in the duplicate set of house keys, which they had previously bestowed on him in recognition of his great efforts, and so that he would feel – to all intents and purposes – an equal member of the Lopez family.

The freezing reception was then continued by Vicenza who, just before the soldier made his way inside Giuseppina's bedchamber, briefed him about their decision to jump straight to the conclusion of the script. That night had to be the epilogue of a tragic play in which he'd been cast by mere chance, the end of what had been a mad tale from the very beginning.

The young conscript would have seen the old mother for the very last time; for his own good, and for their mum's too. Alzheimer's had preceded the Almighty Father, who was probably too busy scratching his own ass.

As he listened to Vicenza's good reasons for abruptly terminating his storytelling position, Nunzio noticed Emilia and Patrizia, who were reeling in a counter-melody of tears and laughter as they admired an old, rumpled photograph. The two women eventually managed to restrain their emotional response and allowed the young conscript to take a look, a quick last peek into their family's riveting intimacy.

It was a black and white snapshot of their mum. It had been taken by the seaside when Giuseppina was only eighteen and still looked as gorgeous as Sophia Loren.

"What do you think, uh?" asked Emilia as her tears rolled over her crumpled smile. "Doesn't my mummy look beautiful?"

"She does," gasped Nunzio. "She truly does!"

XVII

They rang the pharmacy to cancel the order. Her breathing had turned so faint that there wasn't any need for a new oxygen tank. Their exhausted hopes were crushed further by the presence of the Almighty, who turned up inside Giuseppina's bedchamber and took charge of the sick old woman.

As seen through the three sisters' gleaming eyes, God was seated by the dying mother's bed as He held her pendulous hand. The gold-lacquer clock lounged, unwound. It had been left to its own devices from the moment Giuseppina got fed up waiting for nothing, waiting in vain for the Madonna or the Lord to hand her son back to her.

Vicenza, Patrizia and Emilia had serious doubts about the righteousness of their decision to conceal the truth. In hindsight, their plan to protect their mum had gone terribly awry, as the pain they had meant to allay was being calcified in their bones with a vengeance. Moreover, they felt vulnerable and scared stiff at the thought of their mother's reaction once she found out the whole ploy. In heaven, the Lord would gift Giuseppina with a brand-new brain that would immediately let her see how she'd been duped by her shameless daughters.

Dread lived in the three sisters' hearts, for Death would have imminently spilled the beans, thus revealing the faces of the lying bitches that they were.

"Death will snitch on us." The three broken women agonised over this prospect, their quivering arms and words interfused like the branches of three conjoined trees.

"Tell-tale Death will definitely snitch on us. She doesn't talk behind people's backs the way we miscreants do."

"She'll say it right to your face, it's in her nature."

Their mum would have found out the whole thing, including the conspicuous detail about the hospital, which Luigi had never even seen as he was too busy being dead.

During her crossing to the eternal shores, Giuseppina would have heard Death reveal to her: "Hospital, you say? Uh-uh, your son has been dead for years! Dead as a door-nail, honey bunny!"

Due to their untimely contrition, Vicenza, Patrizia and Emilia were expecting a severe punishment. Possibly millennia in Purgatory, where they might be sentenced to eat entire mountain ranges of bullshit before they could make any strides in the Valley of Eden.

*

Being a man of his word, the Almighty helped the undertakers lift the corpse of Giuseppina from her ebbing bed. The Lord flung the old woman out of her home effortlessly – the loaded coffin gliding over the dining room like a tablecloth replete with bread crumbs.

The three sisters jumped in a taxi and followed the hearse all the way to the cemetery. But as the tree- lined path of the crematorium came into sight, they signalled the driver to make a ten-minute diversion ontowards the military mausoleum.

There was still time. Still time for them to tell their mother the whole truth.

They emptied their purses and handed the notes to the undertakers, who took their share and passed on the rest of the tip to the guardians, who were easily coaxed into making an exception and allowing their mum's coffin through the narrow gate of the mausoleum.

All around the multi-storey structure, no image or portrait of the dead marked the niches. Only personal codes, the engraved identification system that the Ministry of Camorra would electronically generate and post out to the next of kin upon confirmation of the loss.

The sisters asked the undertakers to point their mum's coffin up high, towards the third floor, where the niche NA32987 stood out from the rest because of its empty flower pots.

"*Ecce homo*, Mummy!" cried Patrizia.

"They'll look after one another, don't worry!" Emilia tried to comfort her.

While Vicenza whispered, "Rest in peace, both of you!", even though she strongly hoped that the dead would not mind too much saying the occasional prayer for them, for the three sisters who were now completely alone, since their mum too had dumped them with the living.

EPILOGUE

As he stepped inside her bedchamber for the last time, Giuseppina immediately recognised the presence of her son's dear friend Nunzio, as though the fantasy-wrapped train screened their most precious memories against the rampant beasts of oblivion. Right away, the infirm mother looked the young conscript in the eyes and asked him whether he had noticed too. How it had been too many a year since a glowing bride was spotted outside the church in the piazza.

"Since the start of this stupid war," she observed, "everything worth remembering has been forgotten. The beautiful sight of the newlyweds walking down the parvis steps surrounded by smiling faces. The church bells tolling all pains away, and the photographer who calls for each guest to take their place for the family portrait... What could ever be more civil and joyous than two people celebrating their intention to spend the rest of their lives together?"

"Although," Giuseppina sighed pensively, "there is indeed something else that's even more joyous than your wedding day. And that's the day when the Holy Virgin grants you the mercy of having a child. If things don't work out well for a couple, a baby – that's the thing! – will bring you right back to the very start, to one moment prior to the beginning of all time, when all the sounds of the earth and the heavens were part of a single harmony. And the wonderful part of preceding time is that in this place, with no beginning or end in sight, there is absolutely nothing to be afraid of or worry about. Before time, not even the ghost of death could ever lay a finger on you."

Next, as she felt that the train was about to depart, and as a sign of gratitude towards Nunzio, who had been the gentlest of fellow passengers throughout their journey together, the elderly mother wanted to try and return the favour by telling him a tiny little something that perhaps he might find interesting.

The dying woman began her brief account, or rather the telling of a dream she had the previous night, and that had caused her to stay awake ever since in awe.

Giuseppina had dreamt of Luigi, who looked like a saint. Tall and resplendent, he strutted around the wards of the military hospital checking first-hand the conditions of *all* the patients. Furthermore, he'd made copies of the release key for the main lift, and handed one to every single phthisic, so they could finally use them as they pleased, despite any present or future fabrication from the Ministry of Camorra.

"Amen!" Giuseppina burst out with self-content-ment, proud of her son's just and fearless gesture.

Then, as she paused to contemplate the finale of her waning life story, Nunzio started to caress the old wom-an's hair, while his being seemed to implode like a star orphaned by its own core.

He thought it had grown a fair bit.

"Do you know, Mrs Lopez, your hair looks a lot lon-ger today. Honestly!" said the young conscript, as he struggled to blanket the bald patches on the woman's scalp.

Following a few more reverent looks, Nunzio said goodbye to her forehead, her temples, and her sweet face. And simply watched her for the very last time: si-gnora Lopez, in the act of opening the bag brimful with the little thought he'd brought her along with his heart.

"Madonna, they look wonderful!" exclaimed Giusep-pina solemnly.

The whitest mulberries she would ever see.

CONTENTS